"When were you going to tell me?"

Evan's cold tone made Natalie swallow harshly. "When I was ready. I think," she added guiltily. He made a sound of disgust and she lifted her chin, despite knowing in her heart his anger was justified.

"Don't you think I had a right to know?"

Natalie gave a short mirthless laugh. What difference did it make now? He knew, and short of erasing his memory there was nothing she could do about it. Damn her sister for butting her nose into places it didn't belong.

"Natalie…answer me. Don't you think I had a right to know?"

A growing sense of self-preservation sharpened her voice. "Yes, you had a right to know," she agreed. "But if you want me to be honest, I wasn't sure whether or not I was going to tell you and I wish you hadn't found out." His eyes widened at her blunt remark, but she ignored him. "So now you know. Don't worry, I don't want anything from you. You're off the hook, okay? Just go."

Dear Reader,

Fathers come in all shapes and sizes, nationalities and religious preference, but the good ones—the ones who manage to weather the ups and downs of parenting without losing their ability to smile at the end of the day—are unsung heroes. Fathers mold our lives in many different and important ways and sometimes we don't realize the full impact our fathers have made until we're grown with children of our own.

Natalie and Evan's story is one of overcoming preconceived ideas and embracing the possibility of love in all its forms, whether it comes packaged in the traditional box or arrives in a haphazard fashion. I love stories that bring together complete opposites, probably because it mirrors my own life. Like my husband and me, Natalie and Evan are nothing alike, but their attraction is quite undeniable, and when they come together sparks fly. Add a baby to the mix and the ensuing chaos is downright entertaining.

Natalie's story is the first of three connected stories set in the fictitious town of Emmett's Mill. I hope you enjoy reading each of the Simmons sisters' individual tales of living, learning and loving. Just like your own family stories, sometimes there's laughter and sometimes there are tears, but there is always an abundance of love.

Hearing from readers is one of the highlights of my day, so please don't hesitate to let me know what you think of the first in the Simmons sisters trilogy.

You can find me through snail mail at P.O. Box 2210, Oakdale, CA 95361, or through e-mail at my Web site, www.kimberlyvanmeter.com.

Enjoy!

Warmly,

Kimberly Van Meter

FATHER MATERIAL
Kimberly Van Meter

HARLEQUIN®

TORONTO • NEW YORK • LONDON
AMSTERDAM • PARIS • SYDNEY • HAMBURG
STOCKHOLM • ATHENS • TOKYO • MILAN • MADRID
PRAGUE • WARSAW • BUDAPEST • AUCKLAND

ISBN-13: 978-0-373-78178-2
ISBN-10: 0-373-78178-4

FATHER MATERIAL

This edition published by arrangement with Harlequin Books S.A.

www.eHarlequin.com

Printed in U.S.A.

ABOUT THE AUTHOR

An avid reader since before she can remember, Kimberly Van Meter started her writing career at the age of sixteen when she finished her first novel on her mother's old portable typewriter. Currently a journalist (who during college swore she'd never write news), Kimberly has worked for both daily and weekly newspapers. Born and raised in Mariposa, California, Kimberly knows a thing or two about small towns—preferring the quiet, rural atmosphere to the hustle and bustle of a busy city—but she and her husband make their home in Oakdale, which represents a compromise between the two worlds.

The oldest of four siblings and the mother of three children, Kimberly divides her time between soccer games, swim meets, bottle feedings and deadlines.

Books by Kimberly Van Meter

HARLEQUIN SUPERROMANCE
1391—THE TRUTH ABOUT FAMILY

To all the men in my life who understand the true meaning of fatherhood and bear the weight of its responsibility without complaint. You know who you are.

To my sisters, Kristen, Kamrin, Erin, Miranda and Hilary for being amazing women who never fail to make me proud even when we don't always agree.

And to the sisters of my heart, Jaycee and Nicole, for everything in between, sidewise and backward. I'd be lost without you both.

CHAPTER ONE

THE HIGH SUN glinted off the river, its smooth surface broken only by the frothy whitecaps that churned against the rocks hidden beneath, and Natalie Simmons's step faltered as she surveyed its awesome power. Her gaze traveled along the limestone and shale canyon cliffs the river was nestled between and the breath was stolen from her chest.

Holy Mother, she'd never felt so small.

"Amazing, isn't it?" a man with blond hair and a lazy smile asked as he approached, reading her expression. She recovered with a shy nod, accepting his outstretched hand for a quick shake. "It never fails to get me right here every time," he said, knocking on his chest for emphasis. He grinned broadly, showcasing nice, white even teeth that surely made his dentist proud and she found herself smiling back, though she'd never been what could be deemed a flirt by any stretch of the imagination. "Name's Evan. I'll be your guide. What's yours?"

"N-Natalie," she warbled around the dust in her throat. He chuckled as if she weren't the first one to suffer from too much nature all at once and she tried again. "Natalie Simmons."

"Well, Natalie, welcome to Moab. Just sit tight and someone will come to put your stuff with the others. We should be ready to shove off soon."

It was on the tip of her tongue to ask if another bus was coming, as she still hadn't seen Dan anywhere, but Evan the River Guide Guy was gone before she could put the words together. She started toward the cluster of people Evan had pointed to, all the while keeping an eye out for the one person she'd made this trip for.

She couldn't wait to see the look on Dan's face when he saw her. The urge to giggle almost relieved the tightness in her lungs but she contented herself with a secret smile, knowing everything was going to work out.

Another five minutes crawled by and Natalie slapped her thigh in mild annoyance—he was late. Dan was always late.

They used to joke he'd be the type to skid in on one foot to the chapel. She'd, of course, threatened him with bodily harm if he did that on their wedding day and they'd laughed. She swallowed and flinched at the sharp pain that followed but managed to keep her eyes dry. She fingered the pendant around her neck for strength. A gift from her oldest sister before she left for the Peace Corps many years ago, the pendant served to remind her she wasn't here to cry. She'd done enough of that the first month after Dan had left. Now was the time to be proactive. If Dan was going river-rafting, by damn, so was she. She'd show him there were more dimensions to Natalie Simmons than he ever dreamed. Boring, indeed. Predictable, watch this. She was practically a goddamn daredevil, she thought glancing at the river again as if it were a coconspirator, and not the subject of her nightmares a full week running prior to her flight date.

Squaring her shoulders, she jerked at the suitcase as it got stuck on a pebble and moved toward the group with a dogged smile on her face.

Her gaze skipped over the anonymous

faces in an attempt to lock onto the one she knew best, but there was still no sign of him.

"Double-check the knots, Joe," she heard Evan say as he motioned to the slim man who had turned his attention to the rigging on the larger raft that would be used to haul the camp supplies from each location. "I don't mind eating canned beans every night but I'm not sure how well that'll go over with the clients if all our food ends up in the mighty Colorado." Good-natured ribbing and light-hearted laughter followed while Natalie waited for Dan.

She spied a large gnarled piece of wood and, although it didn't look like the most comfortable place to put her rear, at least it wasn't the ground. Out of habit, she glanced at her wrist but her watch was tucked away in her luggage and only a tan line met her eye. Perhaps if Dan didn't show soon, she could ask one of the crew people to radio headquarters or base camp or whatever it was called to find him.

Without meaning to, she found her gaze seeking out the river guide, Evan. He worked quickly and efficiently to get the expedition ready on time, jerking lines to test their strength and helping his colleagues stow luggage on another bargelike raft.

Total eye candy. A dead ringer for Matthew McConaughey if she ever saw one. A candidate for a pinup calendar entitled, "Beach Bum Bachelors." The corners of her lips lifted in amusement as more alliterative calendar names came to mind. Names such as "Randy River Rogues" and "Cute Catches of the Colorado."

When she realized she was staring a bit too intently she tried focusing on something a little less masculine. Besides, as good-looking as he was, he didn't hold a candle to Dan. Of course, she'd never been much for blondes, especially ones with hair that looked perpetually mussed, with the tips bleached white from the sun. It was too bohemian for her tastes. No, she preferred a man with hair as dark and rich as a walnut.

Joe said something just out of Natalie's auditory range and Evan sent a surreptitious glance her way before offering Joe a chuckle.

She stiffened and pretended she didn't notice, then looked out toward the water, entranced by its swift, running surface, until a smiling crew member came to stow her luggage for her.

Feeling oddly vulnerable without something familiar around, she tried shifting to a more comfortable position, but there was no changing the fact her tush was sitting precariously on petrified wood. She didn't have long to move around before Evan started addressing the group and she hurried over to listen.

"Welcome to Wild River Expeditions," he began, rubbing his hands together, his obvious excitement rivaling those of his rafters as they crowded around, eager smiles wreathing their faces. "My name is Evan Murphy and I'll be your guide on this trip." He pointed toward the crew members who were putting the rest of the rafters' luggage on the other rig. "We are here to make your river-rafting experience fun, exciting, something to remember but, more importantly, safe.

"The most valuable skill you can possess to make this trip enjoyable is the ability to listen. The river is a beautiful place but it can be dangerous. You must listen and do as I tell you without hesitation in order to stay safe when we're out there. Together, we'll work as a team to make this the best damn adventure you're ever going to have."

Murmurs of excited agreement rippled

through the small group, but Natalie was too busy watching for another bus and hoping her former fiancé was on it. She frowned when nothing but some indeterminate bird hopped across the path and then flew away. Where was he? Dan was missing all the important stuff. A sliver of irritation followed as her gaze automatically swept the area, again looking for his familiar face.

"Any questions?"

Perhaps he missed his flight or his layover was longer than expected. She sent a worried glance in the direction the bus had gone but there was nothing but scenic nature, pretty as a postcard, staring back.

The hairs rose on the back of her neck and she turned, somehow knowing Evan was staring right at her.

"Any questions?" he asked, his forehead wrinkling in displeasure as if to send home the point that she wasn't listening to the very important things Dan was missing.

"Sorry," she murmured, flushing with embarrassment when the other rafters turned to see who Evan was addressing, knowing she deserved their censure for not paying attention. Panic was beginning to set in and all she could think about was that they were missing the most crucial member of the group.

"All right then, let's get this show on the road!" Evan said, his enthusiasm returning. "You're going to want to change into your swimsuits if you haven't already and grab your hats so we can hop into the boat for some basic instruction before we shove off."

She couldn't let Evan start the trip without Dan. Winding her way through the group as they dispersed to change, Natalie went to tug on Evan's shirt sleeve to catch his attention, but her fingers grazed sun-kissed bare skin instead.

"Oh!" She jerked her hand away as completely inappropriate images of him posing in her fictitious calendar forced their way into her brain. Appalled at herself, she managed to stammer some kind of apology before continuing nervously. "Uh, we can't leave yet. We're missing someone," she said, gesturing desperately at the clipboard in his hand. "Dan Gorlan. He was supposed to be here. Please check your list."

"Gorlan…that name rings a bell." Evan scanned the paperwork, flipping the pages as he searched, and she breathed against the knot in her chest.

Everything was going to be fine. He'd see Dan was missing and he'd send someone to go find him. She'd almost calmed to an acceptable level until he nodded his head, pointing at two names. "Ah, that's right," he said. "I knew I recognized the name. Here it is. Dan Gorlan and Jessica Chambers—canceled. Are they friends of yours?"

Canceled? She wanted to wail at the cosmic cruelty, but she was too stunned by the second bit of information to do more than stare dumbly, her jaw falling slack and her knees wobbling dangerously. "Who's Jessica?" she asked in a guttural whisper.

"I don't know. Maybe one of them got sick. Happens all the time," Evan answered, shifting uncomfortably.

The tears she'd sworn were finished rushed to prove her wrong. He wasn't coming. And even if he had…he'd planned to bring someone else.

"They canceled a few weeks ago," Evan continued awkwardly when she failed to stop staring at him as if he was somehow in on her complete humiliation. "In fact, you and Mrs. Stemming—" he pointed discreetly toward the middle-aged woman wearing an electric blue hat and fussing with her river shoes "—took their places. Otherwise we wouldn't have been able to accommodate your reservations."

Lucky me.

Mortified, Natalie backed away, stumbling on her words as the need to escape swamped her ability to form a coherent sentence.

If she hadn't been choking on a golf-ball-sized clot of misery she would have laughed at the irony. She came all this way for nothing. She blew half her savings on a trip to prove herself to a group of strangers.

And Dan couldn't care less.

The next thing she knew she was moving away, intent on one thing—getting the hell out of there.

CHAPTER TWO

"HOLD ON THERE, are you okay?" Evan called out, startled when she abruptly spun on her heel and practically ran to the supplies raft. Just as she got to the barge, she turned unexpectedly and they almost collided. He skidded to a stop, hands outstretched, and tried again. "Settle down a minute and tell me what's wrong."

"I need my luggage," she answered with a rigid jaw, her face ash-white under the hot sun. "I just need my luggage, please," she repeated with a slight hiccup. When he didn't react quickly enough, she began pawing through the bags with single-minded determination. "I saw it go in here. It's black—"

"Wait," he commanded, alarmed by the sickly shade of her face. "Take a minute to calm down. You don't look so good."

"I'm fine," she insisted, but the shine in her

eyes gave away the presence of tears and her hands were clenched at her sides as if she had a death grip on the last shred of her dignity.

"You look ready to pass out. Wait here," he said, gesturing for her to stay put. He had an idea that might put some color back in her cheeks.

He walked purposefully to his bag and pulled out a clean bandana. After a quick trip to the water's edge, he returned, wringing out the cloth before handing it to her. "Use this to cool down," he instructed, his gut twisting unexpectedly when she peered at him with shy gratitude in her dark hazel eyes, accepting it with a murmured thanks. He looked away quickly, sending his gaze out toward the water and back again until he was certain whatever had just happened to his insides was done.

"I'm sorry," she said, sniffing just a little. "But I can't stay—I thought…well, my friend…he…I just can't."

"Can't what?" he said, gentling his voice. "Start from the beginning. What happened?"

A hiccup followed but she managed to swallow and continue in a stop-and-start manner. "I was going to meet my friend… but it was a…"

"Surprise?" he guessed and she nodded, looking all the more miserable. Something told him her friend Dan wouldn't have been the only one surprised.

"Here's how I see it," he said after she'd handed the bandana back to him. "You shouldn't let your 'friend' ruin your good time."

"That's just it, this isn't what I'd consider a good time," she replied. "This trip was… oh, forget it. I was stupid to think one trip could change anything."

He didn't know what to say. She wasn't the first person to back out of an excursion at such a late date, though admittedly it didn't happen often, but he had a feeling if anyone needed the opportunity to cut loose a little, she did. *It's really none of your business, man.* He ignored the voice in his head and tried one more time, telling himself if that didn't work he'd call for a ride and be on his way.

"If you're truly set on leaving, I'll arrange a car to come and get you but I have to warn you—the trip is nonrefundable this late in the game. Are you prepared to eat a considerable amount of money for nothing? Wouldn't you rather at least have something to show for it?"

His question earned him an uncertain look and he knew he'd hit a nerve. "Who knows, it might even take your mind off your... friend and you could actually have a good time."

Her expression puckered at the word *friend* but his suggestion seemed to have some effect.

"Totally nonrefundable?" she asked, wiping at her nose.

"Sorry...dumb company policy."

Natalie sighed unhappily and her stare dropped to her feet as she seemed to consider the information.

"Boyfriend?" he ventured cautiously, though why he hadn't a clue. He'd long since stopped trying to score with the women on his rig, no matter how oddly adorable they looked in clothes completely ill-suited for such a rugged trip. At thirty-five, he was getting too old to play the games that invariably followed when they realized he wasn't interested in anything more long-term. One woman had actually stalked him for a summer. He gave an imperceptible shudder at the memory but it served to remind him to back off the rafters.

"Ex-fiancé," she whispered, as if saying

the words any louder might make the mortification worse.

"That's rough," he answered, her revelation sending his thoughts tumbling into his own past and he looked away. He knew how it felt to be made a fool. Whoever said time healed all wounds was an idiot in Evan's opinion.

"You wouldn't believe how incredibly stupid I feel right about now," she admitted. She drew hard on her bottom lip just as it started to quiver and Evan couldn't help but commiserate.

"It's his loss," he offered gruffly. "He's probably not worth it."

He heard his name and he knew it was time to shove off. The silence stretched between them until it was almost awkward but he wanted her to stay. Why, he couldn't say and he didn't have time to wonder. "Well? What's it going to be?" he finally asked.

She inhaled deeply and seemed to square her shoulders a bit and the subtle action gave him hope. He made one more push. "Listen, I'm not trying to pry into your business but I know from personal experience riding on the river can go a long way toward soothing a bruised heart." *And a damaged ego.* "Why don't you give it a try? It can't get any worse, right?"

She gave him a derisive look. "I could drown. I'd say that's a bit worse."

"Haven't lost anyone yet."

"There's a first time for everything."

He lifted his hands. "You got me there," he continued, pleased to see a spark of personality popping to life behind her eyes, "but I promise I'll do my best not to start a trend on this particular trip."

She cracked a reluctant smile. "Promise?"

"Absolutely." With that said, he sobered and met her gaze. "So…staying or going?"

She looked out at the river, obviously weighing her decision carefully, and he couldn't help letting his eyes wander. He liked what he saw but she was the last kind of person he needed to be fooling around with—even if she was cute as hell with her sassy short blond hair and long, coltish legs that looked as if they could wrap around a man just like Julia Roberts had in the bathtub scene with Richard Gere in *Pretty Woman.* The random thought made his shorts tighter as the blood rushed from his head to…other places. Annoyance at his reaction colored his voice as he said, "I can't wait much longer. If you really don't want to stay—"

"No," she said quickly, drawing a deep breath and offering a short nod. "You're right. I'm here. The money is already spent. I'll stay."

She offered a tremulous smile as if she expected a pat on the head for her bravery. Instead of feeling aggravated, which he should have been because she'd already thrown him off schedule, his lips tilted upward in a silly grin as he gave her shoulder a friendly rub. "Glad to hear it. For what it's worth, I think you're making the right choice," he said, relieved to note his lower region was returning to normal. Until she graced him with a smile that lit up her face like a Christmas Day parade.

The sincere gratitude he read in those incredible eyes immediately made him wish someone had come along to knock some sense into his head. She wanted to go; he should've just let her. It wasn't his job to talk people into staying. He got paid either way. Suffering under the very real sensation he'd just complicated everything, he grumbled to no one in particular as he raked a hand through his hair.

That woman is gonna be trouble.

What could happen in six days? he scoffed to his internal voice of doom.

Buddy, something tells me, more than you bargained for.

Thanks for the warning. Now, shut up.

He had work to do.

SHE'D MISSED HER CHANCE, she realized as Evan called out last-minute instructions to the crew.

Way to go, she thought a tad sourly as her stomach rolled in a nauseating manner. Why hadn't she backed out when she'd had the chance? Her big defining moment had been engineered so Dan—the two-timing, philandering jerk—could see what an adventurous woman she really was. But Dan was God only knew where with God only knew who and she was left to face a class-four rafting expedition without any witness to her courage. Honestly, what was the point?

She wrestled with the answer because a part of her—obviously the part that hadn't controlled her mouth a moment ago—was still a bit baffled by what had just happened.

Finally, as she was pulling her tankini top over her head in the pseudo private space afforded by a makeshift dressing room, she figured the reason she'd stayed came down to her practical roots. She jerked her shorts back over her hips and buttoned them quickly, then emerged so the next person could change. The simple truth was she could not stand to lose both her dignity and her savings in one day. If she couldn't take back her humiliation, she could at least see this trip through, even if she was so scared she could hardly keep her knees locked for the quake that kept them knocking together like Spanish flamenco castanets at an international dance competition.

Perhaps with any luck the next six days would pass quickly and then she could put the whole rotten mess behind her.

Yeah, right.

She could almost hear a peal of delighted laughter as she envisioned her youngest sister's face when she told the sorry story.

Yes, Nora the irony is *astounding*, she pictured herself saying in the face of her sister's amusement. Dan had booked the trip when they were still together, had even belittled Natalie for her refusal to go; yet, when it came down to the wire, he had chickened out at the last minute and *she'd* seen it through. Unbelievable.

Natalie pulled her short hair into a low ponytail and jammed her hat on her head.

The rafters were starting to head toward the awaiting raft and Natalie knew it was time to go. Evan, along with two crewman, started handing out lifejackets to the ones who were ready and waiting. Evan's hair was a riot of curls that nearly begged for a woman's finger to twirl and play with the soft and inviting mess, and Natalie felt the edge of a smile sneak up on her. She made her way slowly, so as to give herself enough time to continue the mental pep talk she had going in her head, and kept her gaze focused on Evan. For some reason keeping him within her sights made her feel less jittery. At least he'd seemed kind and, right about now, that's all that mattered. She really didn't care why it made her feel better because frankly, at the moment she didn't care much about anything.

CHAPTER THREE

"OKAY, THE FIRST DAY we're going to take it easy on you," said Evan, grinning as Natalie's group, eight in all, eagerly awaited instruction. "But tomorrow, you're in for one hell of a ride!" The group started applauding and cheering, except for Natalie, whose guts pitched at the very idea of such a promise. He continued with the same enthusiasm, jumping down from the small rock he'd been standing on to motion toward the boat. "So, let's get this show on the road."

Excitement, adventure, excitement, adventure, Natalie kept saying the words over and over again in her head as she climbed aboard. Perhaps if she kept saying the words she'd actually start believing them. *Fat chance*, she answered herself just as the raft dipped with the jostling weight of the other rafters.

"Are you sure this is safe?" she asked, her

heart rate increasing to an unhealthy speed. A few puzzled looks came her way, and she gave a wan smile. "I'm a little nervous," she murmured. *Understatement of the year.* Natalie swallowed and gripped the sides of her seat so hard her knuckles whitened and she thought she might actually crack the seat.

The woman Evan identified as Mrs. Stemming smiled generously and patted her knee. "Oh, dear, don't worry. Evan is the best guide there is. We couldn't be safer. I promise you that."

"So, you've done this before?" Natalie managed to ask once her tongue started working again.

Mrs. Stemming shook her head. "Nope. First time. But I've known Evan and Johnny since they were both knee high to a grasshopper and when it comes to the safety of others, those boys don't cut corners."

Boys? "Who's Johnny?" she asked.

"Oh, Johnny is Evan's older brother. He goes by John now that he's all grown up but he'll always be Johnny to me."

"Yeah? So how do you know Evan?" she asked, loosening her grip on the seat long enough to rub her palms against her thighs.

"His mom was one of my best friends before cancer took her much too young," she answered without a moment's hesitation. "Anyway, I've always wanted to do something a little daring and Evan suggested—the little devil!—a rafting trip. Can you imagine? A rafting trip at my age? Well, nonetheless, he talked me into it and here I am. Isn't it glorious? Who knew Utah was so beautiful."

Natalie smiled at Mrs. Stemming's girlish giggle despite the cold knot of fear that had slid from her throat to her stomach. "Well, that's sweet…but how do you know he's safe?"

Mrs. Stemming appeared nonplussed, as if Natalie was deliberately being obtuse, and answered with a shake of her head. "Because he's never had an accident before, silly. Now stop worrying and get ready to have some fun!"

Natalie wanted to tell the woman that she would have felt much more secure if the raft had seat belts and remained on dry land, but figured she ought to just keep her mouth shut and hold on for dear life.

"We're going to float down the river a ways before we hit some nice little waves, more like rolling hills," said Evan, maneuvering himself to the back of the raft. "Now, take your oar and slide it into the water, get the feel of the river on the oar…that's it."

Evan's encouraging tone soon had everyone working in concert to help propel the boat along the river. Despite wanting to throw up, Natalie found the motion oddly soothing as they slid easily with the current.

"See? Isn't this fun?" shouted Mrs. Stemming over the sound of the water. "This is what I call living!"

Natalie flashed Mrs. Stemming a shy smile before returning her attention to the oar work. Perhaps this wouldn't be so bad after all. If only Dan was there to see her, she thought then deliberately stomped on the beginnings of similar thoughts. Dan had obviously moved on and she wasn't invited. She blinked hard and forced her mind to empty of everything but the focus needed to move her oars with her companions.

They glided along the river for about an hour before they hit the first big wave. Although Evan probably wouldn't have classified it as big, Natalie thought they were about to be smashed to bits against the rocks. Clenching the oar in her hand, she only had a split second to send a prayer skyward before the boat was in the roiling water.

"Steady now," he called out. "We're going to glide right over this little wave. Hold on! Woo-hoo!"

The raft quickly crested the small set of waves and a cool blast of breath-stealing spray danced on their faces. Natalie hadn't realized she had squeezed her eyes shut until Mrs. Stemming nudged her.

"You're missing out on the beautiful scenery, dear, open your eyes!"

Natalie only had time to nod quickly before the next wave hit and she had to concentrate on keeping her seat and working her oar. The sound of Mrs. Stemming's enthusiastic "wooo-heee!" made her grin a little easier and for a heartbeat she forgot that she had booked this trip for entirely different reasons than everyone else.

"Good job, guys," Evan said, looking the part of beach babe and hippie love-child without even realizing it. She should've been turned off, as she never found that type of man attractive, but at the moment he was one hundred percent appealing. Natalie scowled at her own thoughts. Evan was so…not Dan.

His voice, carrying over the sounds of the river and the rafters, continued and she realized if she didn't start paying attention she might end up in the water. But, as it turned out, her concern was unwarranted as the river evened out for an easy glide.

"Oh, it's just breathtaking, isn't it!" Mrs. Stemming gushed, prompting a vigorous nod from Natalie. "Absolutely stunning!"

It was truly something she'd never thought to experience outside of the pages in the books housed at the library. For a moment, she felt removed from the emotional trauma she'd suffered only one short hour ago and felt the stirrings of actual enjoyment. She let a true smile form on her lips and stole a glance at Evan while he guided the boat with ease.

As Nora would say "What a hottie!" A woman could make a long, satisfying meal out of just skimming the sculpted planes of his lean frame, devouring him inch by delicious inch. Her cheeks colored but it didn't stop her from continuing to enjoy the view. His square jaw hinted at a stubborn streak, she noted with interest, and she wondered what sort of things made him dig his heels in and refuse to yield. But as he offered a grin at something someone said to him, her breath stopped in her chest and she knew why he made her insides feel strange.

It was the smile—lazy and inviting at the same time, and damn hard to ignore. Feeling mildly relieved at having deciphered why she gravitated toward him, she trailed her fingers through the water, privately delighting in the crisp temperature.

Shaking the frizz of gray curls free from her hat, Mrs. Stemming made a big show of taking in the scenery by exclaiming at the rocks protruding from the riverbed and the birds flying overhead.

"Oh, I wish I had taken this trip years ago," she said, an air of wistful yearning in her voice. "It's amazing how quickly life passes you by when you're not paying attention to all the things that matter." After resting her hat on her knee, Mrs. Stemming gave Natalie a tap on the shoulder. "So, are we having fun yet or what?"

EVAN HEARD THE question posed by the venerable Mrs. Stemming and was curious to the answer as well. Without seeming too obvious, Evan positioned his body so that he could hear the conversation a little better.

"Well, the scenery is certainly very pretty," Natalie offered, seeming to enjoy sharing with the older woman, not that she'd have much of a chance to refuse, he thought with a private chuckle. Gladys Stemming was a force of nature. "It's a lot different from what I'm used to."

"And where is that, dear?"

"Emmett's Mill, California."

"Why, that's just around the bend from where I'm from!" Mrs. Stemming exclaimed happily. "Imagine that! It's such a small world."

Evan's foot slipped with an embarrassing thud but he recovered before anyone noticed. Emmett's Mill was only an hour from the ranch he shared with his brother, John.

An unexpected thrill chased the acknowledgment but he worked hard to stamp it down. She was his client. He had no business thinking of her in any other way. But…there was something about Natalie that he found intriguing. No harm there, he supposed. Intriguing people helped make a trip interesting. He continued to listen.

"Does your family still live there?"

Natalie chuckled wryly. "Oh, yes. You'd

have to sandblast my dad out of Emmett's Mill. My younger sister, Nora, lives just around the block from me, but my older sister, Natasha, we call her Tasha for short, moved away. She's in the Peace Corps so she lives all over the place. I'm not exactly sure where she is right now."

"The Peace Corps? How exciting," Mrs. Stemming murmured and Natalie offered a distracted nod. "Do you see her often?"

Natalie shook her head. "Not enough. She comes home for brief visits now and then but she mostly sends postcards. Each tour is three years so it's hard to get away."

Mrs. Stemming clucked at her admission but, as if sensing the subject was a sensitive one, she refrained from asking more questions. Unfortunately, catching a tiny glimpse into Natalie's personal life only made Evan want to know more.

Mrs. Stemming copied Natalie's move and leaned over to trail her fingers in the cool water. "Oh! That's nippy, but it feels good." After dabbing her forehead she changed directions, saying, "I couldn't help but notice you were a tad upset earlier…."

Natalie shrugged as if whatever had been

upsetting was over, but Evan caught the corners of her lips turning down and knew otherwise. When she started talking, he strained to listen.

"Actually, I was supposed to meet my… boyfriend here, but I guess we got our wires crossed," she admitted, stumbling on the word *boyfriend*. Although Mrs. Stemming had been satisfied with Natalie's answer, Evan knew she had just lied. Whoever this Dan Gorlan was, he must have hurt her pretty bad. Evan recognized the signs. When his fiancée had left him for his best friend, his world had imploded and he'd walked away from everything—ambition, dreams, goals— with only a single purpose: survival. John hadn't agreed with his methods but Evan hadn't much cared. He'd done what he had to to get through the day without curling up in a useless ball.

With a silent sigh, he pushed aside his musings and any other inappropriate thoughts concerning Natalie and focused on getting the rafters to the next destination, their first camp.

CHAPTER FOUR

BY THE TIME they reached the area where they were to camp for the night, Natalie had begun to enjoy herself.

Mistaking her quiet for boredom, Mrs. Stemming patted her shoulder before disembarking and said with a wink, "Don't worry, dear, tomorrow will be full of the huge waves and heart-stopping drops that you young folk love! Just you wait!"

Before she had time to stop the quake that started in her left knee at the very thought, Evan was at her elbow to help her out. "Whoa there, no sense in going for a dip before nightfall, you'll freeze your little behind off."

Natalie flashed him a grateful smile and accepted his hand. "I guess I don't have my river legs yet," she managed to say despite the fact his touch sent a different type of tremor rumbling through her body. "I'll admit I'm a bit glad to be on the ground again."

Evan flashed a knowing smile and gestured toward the encampment, where his crew had already set up their tents.

"Wow, how did they manage that?" Natalie waved a hand at the small assortment of tents pitched into the soft sand.

"The crew always go ahead of the group so everything is ready when they arrive."

Natalie's neon orange pup tent stood out among the earthy colors of everyone else's tents and she wished she'd taken up Nora's offer to borrow hers. She looked over at Evan just in time to see his expression crinkle in amusement.

"It was on sale," she said, raising her chin.

He lifted his hands and chuckled. "Nothing beats a sale. At least no one will mistake your tent for theirs."

She looked at him, startled. "Does that ever happen?" Visions of a stranger stumbling into her shelter in the dead of night after a nature call made her wish it came with a padlock. Evan's smile widened, causing her to prompt him nervously. "Well? Do they?"

He laughed, winking as he slowly walked in the opposite direction toward the crew. "Sometimes. But usually it's by invitation."

Natalie inhaled sharply as she caught his meaning. "Oh!" she said in a soft tone, casting a quick look around to see if anyone else had caught his comment and to gauge whether or not there were any "wanderers" rafting with them. Aside from two couples who were already enamored with each other, the rest of the rafters were older and seemed less inclined to flirt their way into her bedroll. Except Evan. He didn't appear much older than she, perhaps only by a few years, and as far as she could tell, he wasn't attached.

What did that matter? She turned and caught a covert glimpse as he laughed easily with his crew buddies, the sound coaxing a reluctant smile. The feeling as her mouth curved was surprising. For a split second her heart wasn't dragging on her chest, as if a lead weight was trapped inside her rib cage, and she'd almost enjoyed it. But as quickly as it came, reality soon followed and the motion faded. Unlike everyone else, she hadn't come to experience an adrenaline-soaked adventure. She'd come to convince her wayward fiancé—*excuse me*, ex-fiancé—that they were meant to be together, but she'd failed and she was alone. How truly pathetic.

Disgusted with herself and her inability to just suck it up and move on, as either of her sisters would've done in this situation, she excused herself from the group and sought the solitude of the foreign—but ultimately breathtaking—surroundings. She hoped she didn't get bit by some mean-tempered reptile for her troubles.

Within moments she'd found herself a secluded spot away from the camp and, after thoroughly checking the area for creepy crawlies, she planted her behind on a flat rock. Huddled against the rapidly chilling breeze, she wrapped her arms around her knees and watched as the sun slowly descended beyond the horizon.

Nora had been right. As far as bad ideas went, this one took the cake. She drew her knees up and hugged them against her chest for warmth. A mournful sigh escaped as she wallowed in a healthy dose of self-pity. She had no one but herself to blame, although the knowledge only made her feel worse. Natalie was thankful for the quickening darkness. She didn't think she could handle the idea of anyone feeling sorry for her. She was doing enough of that for herself.

So, what now? was the question.

She sighed and a shudder rippled through her. Well, one thing was for sure, she couldn't spend all night perched on this rock. If she didn't unfurl herself right this second, she might never. Her legs were cramped from the position and her butt was completely numb.

The minute she reintegrated into the group, going straight to the fire pit to warm her frozen body, Mrs. Stemming pounced with the forceful friendliness of a lonely matron.

"And just where'd you take yourself off to, dear?" she asked. "I was about to send Evan out after you."

Thank heaven for small favors. The last thing she wanted was Evan's pity. Forcing a smile, she answered with as much nonchalance as she could muster under the circumstances. "Just a little nature call is all."

At that Mrs. Stemming hooted, a mischievous twinkle in her eyes as she cried in mock alarm. "Oh, lands alive! Imagine if he'd happened upon you when you were 'indisposed.' A person could die of embarrassment."

She offered a small smile in response but knew if that were actually possible she'd have keeled over the moment she heard Dan had skipped out. A sharp pain brought sudden tears to her eyes, but she covered by pretending the smoke was irritating them. Mrs. Stemming continued to chatter like a magpie but even the older woman's entertaining prattle couldn't change the fact that she felt like the biggest wet blanket.

Fortunately, it was mostly a one-sided conversation and only required the occasional murmured response until Mrs. Stemming drew a deep breath after a particularly long monologue and focused on Natalie with the same enthusiasm.

"Now, tell me what made you decide to take this trip before we get a mouthful of Jonesy's famous chili and can't speak for the fire on our tongues."

At Mrs. Stemming's expectant expression, Natalie found herself unsure of where or how to begin. It wasn't as if she was fulfilling a life's dream by risking her life on some raft with people she hardly knew. The minute the thought came to her, she was immediately shamed by her attitude. But facts were facts, and now that she'd come to her senses—too late—Natalie didn't feel up to sharing. Instead she opted for a variation of the truth and hoped Mrs. Stemming didn't see right through her.

"Well, it's like I said earlier…I was going to meet someone here and he wasn't able to make it," Natalie said, choosing to watch the dancing flames in the fire pit instead of facing the genuinely nice older woman. Natalie was afraid if she saw a hint of knowing in her eyes, she wouldn't be able to stop the tears that were already too close for comfort anytime she thought of or mentioned Dan. "And, well, he couldn't make it."

Natalie tried a self-deprecating laugh but it came out sounding rather pathetic so she stopped trying to make the effort.

"Hmmm…is he *really* your boyfriend?"

Startled, Natalie could only stare. She'd never been a good liar, but right at that moment she'd have given a kidney or something to offer a well-oiled whopper. Fortunately, Mrs. Stemming saved her the effort of stammering some semblance of a reasonable falsehood when she chuckled softly and patted her knee.

"It doesn't take a rocket scientist to see that someone had their heart broken. When did you break up, dear?"

Was it tattooed on her forehead? *I was dumped by my fiancé and now he's shacking up with some bimbo named Jessica? Please ask for details—I love talking about it.*

"Three months ago," Natalie found herself answering in spite of her decision to nicely, but firmly, tell Mrs. Stemming to back off.

"Well, everything happens for a reason. I know advice like that always comes off sounding trite and it's the last thing you want to hear anyway, but it's the truth either way you slice it."

Natalie turned to regard Mrs. Stemming. "But how do you know that he wasn't 'the one'? What if I just let him slip through my fingers?"

Mrs. Stemming made a small clucking noise at Natalie's fears. "Darling, call it fate, call it the hand of God, whatever…the bottom line is if this man was 'the one' he'd be here with you now."

Even though the chatter of the other rafters surrounded her, all she heard was the wisdom of Mrs. Stemming's words. Wiping away the moisture that had gathered at the corners of her eyes, she reluctantly nodded. "I guess that's one way of looking at it, but I'd be lying if I said I didn't still hope he was the one."

Mrs. Stemming nodded in understanding, taking a moment to receive a bowl of hot chili, cornbread and corn on the cob from Jonesy. She gave the oversized man an appreciative wink before returning to Natalie. "If he's the one, fate will put him back in your path. Don't fret. Everything works out for the best in the end. Now, enough talk of such depressing things. We're here to have a fabulous time and I suggest we start with this delicious plate of good stuff!"

With that Mrs. Stemming dug into her chili like a woman who hadn't eaten in a week, exclaiming over each mouthful and encouraging Natalie to do the same.

Despite the sadness she felt, Natalie took a healthy bite of her own chili, nearly choking as the spices alternately delighted and charred her tongue. "Holy cow, that's spicy!"

Jonesy, overhearing her, gave her a wide-mouthed grin, as if the proof of his culinary expertise was strengthened by the sound. He then ladled another scoop of the stuff into a bowl for another rafter.

"Yowza," Natalie gasped, opening and closing her mouth like a fish out of water in an attempt to cool the raging fire on her tongue. "There ought to be a warning label on this stuff."

Mrs. Stemming only laughed and took another bite. "This is what I call living, dear!"

With Mrs. Stemming as a dinnermate, Natalie was hard-pressed to remain in her state of melancholy and actually began to relax. Following dinner Evan regaled the group with stories of past excursions, promising a big day on the river and sending butterflies smashing into her rib cage at the very thought. But even so, she smiled more than she had in months and it felt good.

Steve, the other river guide steering the second group of rafters, announced, amidst groans and pleas for more stories from Evan, that he was going to turn in for the night. Slapping Evan good-naturedly on the back he made his way toward his own tent and disappeared.

"As much as I'd love to continue, we should all turn in. We rise early tomorrow and you're going to need your rest for what we have in store for you guys," Evan said, following a particularly comical story about Jonesy and an inquisitive lizard that had managed to find its way into the big man's sleeping bag one year.

Yawns and nods of agreement followed Evan's announcement and Mrs. Stemming rose stiffly from her chair. "I don't know about you but I'm beat! I never thought I'd see the day when I looked forward to crawling into a sleeping bag to conk out on the ground. But that's exactly where I'm headed!" Shaking her head at the wonder of it, Mrs. Stemming disappeared into the dark to her own tent.

As she yawned herself, Natalie watched as Evan walked to the boat to ensure it was secured and then, in a move that surprised her, hopped in. Joe walked by, carrying a bag of trash to load into their supplies boat, and she gestured toward Evan to ask what he was doing.

"Oh, Evan always sleeps with the boat," he answered without breaking stride. She wanted to ask why, but Joe had already moved out of range and she didn't want to distract him further.

Although her eyes burned, she found herself heading toward the boat. The sound of a sleeping bag zipping closed made her imagination kick into gear as if someone else had taken control. Sweats or pajama bottoms? Boxers or briefs? Her cheeks flared with heat and she was thankful it was dark. Still, she didn't alter her course and soon she was standing right before him.

"Natalie?" he asked, barely able to make out her slender form in the pale moonlight. "Something wrong?"

"Uh, no," she answered, though there was the barest of hesitation in her reply. "I… wondered…well, Joe said you always sleep in the boat and I wondered why."

"The guides usually sleep with the rigs."

"It doesn't look very comfortable."

He chuckled, pulling at his sleeping bag so

he could sit up. "It's not the Hyatt but it's not bad, either. You get used to it."

"It's amazing what we get used to, isn't it?" she asked softly, though Evan sensed she was talking about something other than his sleeping quarters.

"You sure everything's all right?"

She inhaled sharply as if she'd just realized what she'd revealed and a forced chuckle followed. "Yeah. Everything's fine. I'm sorry to have bothered you. Good night, Evan."

The sound of retreating footsteps told him she'd left. Once he was certain she wasn't going to double back, he settled into a comfortable position, tucking his hands behind his head so he could enjoy the beauty of the night sky. Usually, he could lose himself in the endless sheet of diamond-studded skies, but tonight he was distracted. Try as he might he couldn't stop thoughts of Natalie from intruding on his quiet time.

Whoever this Dan character was, he wasn't very bright. Natalie seemed like the kind of woman a man liked to keep. Not him, of course, but someone.

And damn it, why not him, he countered as if in challenge to his own counsel. As if he didn't know good and well why he wasn't the right person for a woman like Natalie. Why he didn't even dare try something casual with her. *Because it wouldn't be enough and casual was all he had to offer.*

And there it was, folks. He tipped an imaginary hat to his ex-fiancée with a sardonic twist of his mouth. *Thanks for the memories, sweetheart.* Ten years was a long time to nurse a wound John liked to tell him, but each time he felt himself getting close to a woman, invariably memories of Hailey intruded to ruin whatever he had going. Eventually, he learned it was just easier on everyone to keep off that beaten path.

Still, as he looked into the night sky and found the moon staring down at him with its usual indifference, he wondered if there would ever come a time when he could look at a woman and welcome a deeper attraction, something that went beyond the physical. A long moment passed, heavy with his own reflections, until he groaned and twisted on his side. He must be getting old. Ignoring everything except the need for sleep he closed his eyes. The only thing he had to offer Natalie was more baggage, and by the sounds of it, she was already packing her fair share. A sad chuckle escaped him as he drifted off. *What a more perfect pair as we…*

CHAPTER FIVE

NATALIE EMERGED from her tent, dressed but not quite ready to face the day.

Evan was directing the group to suit up for the biggest day on the river. The butterflies that had been present and accounted for yesterday returned with their big brothers to wreak havoc on her nerves and intestinal lining. Rubbing her stomach as it gurgled its distress, she cast a look at Mrs. Stemming, who was singing an off-key ditty about some unfortunate soul and a bottle of rum.

"Oh, you look positively pale as a ghost, dear!" she said, though the open concern in her face was outshone by the excitement in her voice. "Natalie! Do yourself a favor and relax! You're entirely too serious for a young gal. If you're not careful, you'll give yourself an ulcer before you're forty."

Natalie smiled despite the roiling of her

stomach. Before she could say another word, Mrs. Stemming had clasped her hand and tugged her toward the boat. Natalie had little choice but to follow after the older woman or she'd risk losing an appendage.

"Today is going to be the ride of your life," Evan promised once everyone had assembled by the boat. "But you must remember the safety tips we went over yesterday. Double-check the clasps on your safety vests. You must listen to your guide. That's me," he added helpfully, smiling as the group chuckled. "And if by some freak chance you happen to fall out of the boat, remember to try and lie flat, feet up. Your vest will keep you afloat and by lying flat you'll skim over the tops of some of the rocks."

Natalie felt a lump bobble in her throat. *Did people really fall out of the boat?*

As if the unspoken question had just flashed across her forehead in neon colors, Evan answered, "Yes, on occasion, we have had people involuntarily leave the boat, but we've never lost anyone and I don't intend to today. We have crew members flanking the river with ropes in hand at the wild spots, just in case someone gets into trouble."

Mrs. Stemming poked her with an elbow.

"Isn't that exciting? The possibility of danger, the thrill of you versus nature, the—"

"No," Natalie breathed, cutting off Mrs. Stemming's nattering and hoping a bolt of lightning would snake out of the sky and strike her down before she had to step foot in that cursed boat. "I think I'm going to pee my pants," she squeaked, earning a full-throated guffaw from Mrs. Stemming.

"Go ahead, dear. We're going to be wet pretty soon anyway. No one will notice!"

She had just enough time to shoot an appalled look Mrs. Stemming's way before Evan was grasping their forearms and helping them take their spots so they could shove off.

No turning back now. Gripping her oar a little tighter, she gave Mrs. Stemming a shaky smile and sent a prayer skyward that she was not going to be one of the terminally unlucky who happened to take a dunk in the drink.

They floated easily enough, giving Natalie's butterflies a chance to calm down, but just as she started to truly relax the river made a sharp and abrupt change in temperament. Going from smooth and tranquil to rough and choppy in seconds, Natalie only had time to grip her oar and listen for Evan's commands.

"Here comes a good one," Evan shouted over the roar of the river. "Left side, paddle now!"

Jolted by the urgency in Evan's voice at her back and the sight of the frothing water they were rapidly approaching, Natalie threw all her strength into paddling as directed. Fear and adrenaline pumped in equal parts through her body but Natalie could only paddle as if her life depended on it. She could hear Mrs. Stemming laughing behind her and wondered if the woman had lost her crackers. *Who in their right mind thought this was fun?*

"Good job, now right!"

Natalie lifted her oar out of the water and the right-side rafters began to paddle furiously, the boat lifting as a wave sent them hurtling down the chute like a greased hog. They crested one wave after another, until Natalie was drenched from the spray, her hair plastered to her face and her chest heaving from the exertion of paddling. But somewhere between being so scared she thought she really might make good on her claim of peeing in her shorts to facing down yet another seemingly monstrous rapid, a laugh full of exhilaration escaped from her lips and she realized in amazement that she was actually enjoying herself.

Throwing herself into the task of paddling, Natalie was stripped of her ability to worry, her built-in desire for perfection and order— she was free to just do as the moment dictated and it felt good.

Amid the laughter of the other rafters, Natalie heard the whoops and hollers of Mrs. Stemming above the rest and joined along with her.

The water began to smooth out and Natalie had time to turn to Mrs. Stemming and give her a bright smile.

"See? What did I tell you?" the older woman said, pushing chunks of wet, gray hair from her eyes, her voice breathless from exertion. "And this is just the beginning."

The beginning? Before Natalie could fully complete the thought, Evan was barking commands again. Something along the lines of "big drops" were all she could hear from his shouted words. Natalie whipped her head back to the front and had time to utter half a gasp before the raft plunged nearly thirty feet down a rapid that put the sections they had just traveled to shame.

Shrieking as her stomach dropped in the same fashion as their raft, Natalie could not make out Evan's command, but followed the lead of the other rafters on her side and began paddling like crazy.

Another drop and Natalie's heart threatened to stop but Mrs. Stemming was laughing like a hyena.

"Right! Left! Hold on!"

Natalie felt the raft surge up as another rapid did its best to smash the raft and its occupants against the rocks and in the next moment she was teetering on the edge of the raft, milliseconds away from kissing the current. Flailing her arms wildly and using muscles she didn't know she had, she wrenched herself away from the edge, using her oar as leverage. *Ha!* She hadn't gone into the river! Turning to grin victoriously at Mrs. Stemming, she was horrified to see the spot where the old lady had been hooting gleefully at every crest was empty.

"Mrs. Stemming!" she screeched, turning to search the water for signs of the older woman. Where was she? What if she was being smashed against the rocks? Surely her old bones wouldn't be able to withstand such a battering.

"Evan! Mrs. Stemming—" Twisting in her seat to send a frantic look to Evan she saw that he was already in motion. He quickly found the bobbing figure and motioned to his spotters situated on the rocks. Biting her knuckle against the fear that the older woman had died in her quest for a little adventure, Natalie could only hope the spotters grabbed her before she hit another patch of wild water.

Luck seemed to be on the older woman's side as she managed to grasp the towrope thrown to her and hang on while they pulled her to safety from the river's edge. Unaware that she had been holding her breath while the spotters reeled the older lady in like an orange-vested salmon, Natalie exhaled forcibly once she was safely out of the water. Mrs. Stemming gave a shaky wave at the passing rafters and Natalie fought tears of relief.

The rafters let out a cheer, a few even whistling in appreciation of Mrs. Stemming's adventure, but Natalie was ready to get off the boat.

Unfortunately, she didn't have the luxury

of pulling the brake and jumping off at the next stop. The next set of rapids hit and Evan's voice, strong and sure, told them to look alive.

Strange choice of words, she thought darkly, sinking her oar into the water and slicing it with strong strokes. Soon, the water calmed again and Evan began directing the rafters toward a sandy beach area. Using the muscles of eight people, the raft made its way to the shore and Evan jumped out to secure the line that would anchor the boat to the river's edge.

"Wasn't that *freaking* amazing?" a sandy-haired girl who looked to be all of fourteen exclaimed as they exited the raft. "I want to do that again!"

Natalie met the dubious expression of the older man, presumably the girl's father judging by the exhausted look on his face, and smiled at her exuberance, but wasn't ready to agree.

Natalie got the impression, as the man and his daughter walked to the camp area, that the man didn't get to spend much time with his daughter and the rafting trip had been her idea. Well, at least she wasn't the only one who had taken this trip for someone else, she thought wearily.

Wanting to have a few words with Evan, she was disappointed to see that he was already off the boat and heading toward the camp. Realizing he was probably going to check on Mrs. Stemming, Natalie hurried after him. The shock of seeing the plucky older lady bob down the river was soon replaced by the need to verify that she was, indeed, all right.

"Evan, wait," she called out after him, pleased when he slowed his step and turned. Once she had caught up, she smiled her thanks. "I just want to make sure she's okay."

Evan nodded and went straight to the area where the spotters would have deposited the older woman until he arrived.

Fearing the worst, Natalie steeled herself against the possibility that the unsinkable Mrs. Stemming may have been seriously wounded. But the moment she laid eyes on the woman, she realized she should have known better. In the short time she'd known Mrs. Stemming, she should have known nothing short of the apocalypse could keep that woman down.

"There you are!" the older woman said,

struggling to rise in spite of the goose-egg-sized bruise forming on her right kneecap. Brushing away Natalie's concern and Evan's rush to assist her, she said, "I'm just fine. A minor scrape is all. Now don't you dare tell me that I can't ride because of it!"

Natalie stared in surprise. After nearly drowning, the woman wanted to go at it again? It was official: Mrs. Stemming *had* lost her crackers.

"But Mrs. Stemming, just look at that bruise!" Natalie protested, gesturing to the motley purple and bluish spot swelling her knee. "You're lucky you didn't bust a leg or something." Turning to Evan for reinforcements she demanded he explain to the older woman why she shouldn't ride. "Go on, Evan, tell her."

Evan wanted to laugh. The expressions of both women were equally endearing and dangerous. Mrs. Stemming hadn't suffered any broken bones during her solo ride down the Colorado, but the swelling on her knee would make it uncomfortable for her later. If he told her she had to stay grounded, he'd never hear the end of it. The woman knew where he lived.

Apparently realizing by his silence that he

did not readily agree with her own assessment of Mrs. Stemming's ability to reboard the raft, Natalie sent a formidable stare his way. "She's obviously hurt. I would imagine there are liability issues that you must contend with if you allow her to ride when she's already injured."

Under normal circumstances, he would have been annoyed at having a client talking to him in such a manner, but he was too distracted by the way Natalie's hazel eyes changed color with the force of her conviction. Her cheeks were flushed, adding more color than usual to her features, and her hair was beginning to curl in wild sections around her face as it dried in the heat of the sun. Shifting in his place, he squinted at Mrs. Stemming as if deliberating her condition before he delivered his verdict. "Let me see you walk on it," he finally said.

Thrusting out her chin, Mrs. Stemming took two brave steps forward, but Evan could tell by the way she bit her lip and favored her uninjured side that it was causing her pain.

"Oh, pooh," Mrs. Stemming said, doing a little hop to relieve the pressure on her injured knee before he steadied her with his shoulder. Looking up, she said with a sigh full of regret and disappointment, "I guess Natalie's right…I am sidelined."

Natalie let out an audible sound of relief. "I think that's a wise choice, Mrs. Stemming."

"I suppose," she said glumly.

"Tell you what," Evan offered, unable to stand Mrs. Stemming's downcast expression. "Take it easy for the rest of the evening. I'll bet by tomorrow you'll be just fine. With a little ice and a few aspirins, you should be able to ride first thing in the morning."

Mrs. Stemming's face lit up and when he looked quickly to gauge Natalie's reaction she rewarded him with an approving smile that told him she agreed with the compromise.

"Sounds good to me," Mrs. Stemming said, gesturing toward the camp area where everyone else was stretching cramped limbs and sore muscles. "In the meantime, let's see what that Jonesy has cooked up for us for dinner. I, for one, am starved!"

Another smile found its way to Natalie's lips and she moved to help Evan shoulder Mrs. Stemming's weight. He probably could have handled it on his own, but it made Natalie feel good to lend a hand.

Evan settled Mrs. Stemming into a foldout camping-style chair and propped her leg up with another before going to talk with the other river guide.

"That's a good man right there," Mrs. Stemming declared, gesturing to Evan as he talked with his crew. Natalie shrugged as if she wasn't in a position to say one way or another, because honestly she wasn't. "And, he's single as the day is long. Just needs the right woman in my opinion," she added, looking meaningfully at Natalie.

"You are transparent, you know that?" When Mrs. Stemming only grinned, Natalie shook her head even as a low chuckle followed. "I hate to break it to you but he's not my type." When Mrs. Stemming started to protest, she continued gently but firmly, saying, "Besides, I'm in love with Dan. I told you that."

"Yes, dear, but is this Dan character in love with you?"

Tears sprang to Natalie's eyes and she drew back. *That hurt.* Inhaling deeply, she willed the tears to recede and managed a smile. "He's just a little confused right now.

He'll come around. I'm sure of it." She added with a small, forced laugh, "Dan is the artistic type. Sometimes they need to lose something before they realize they really miss it."

"We're not talking about a pair of socks, honey," Mrs. Stemming said gently. "We're talking about a woman's heart—your heart. Does he deserve a second chance at breaking it?"

Natalie's breath hitched in her chest and she realized she had to get away from the wisdom of Mrs. Stemming. Rising on wobbly feet, she managed to smile despite the feeling of her heart cracking in familiar places and stammer something about needing a nature break. She knew if she stayed a moment longer she wouldn't be able to stop the tears that were brimming under the surface. The thought of breaking down in front of anyone, much less a group of strangers, was not something she was willing to entertain.

Trudging past the group of rafters toward a spot that seemed to offer a modicum of privacy, Natalie made her way up a steep incline that leveled out to reveal a glorious view of the Colorado.

Natalie took a seat, not caring that the red, claylike dust covering the rocks would probably stain her jean shorts forever, and tried to relieve the aching pressure that pulsed behind her eyes and squeezed her chest with each beat. The river cut a deep gorge into the sides of the canyon as it snaked its way through the Utah landscape, its beauty both stark and awe-inspiring. From her vantage point, the sunlight sparkling from the water's surface flashed like precious stones winking from beneath and Natalie wondered how she of all people had come to be here.

The tightness in her chest lessened enough for her to take a deep breath, but her heart still ached with the knowledge that Dan probably wasn't coming back.

Although Natalie had never laid eyes on the woman, she was willing to bet her eyeteeth that Dan's mystery woman was a brunette with curves that could stop a Mack truck and a wild spirit that convention couldn't contain. In other words: the exact opposite of her.

Even her name was fun and flirty. *Jessica.* Not anything like the solid name of *Natalie.* Solid and boring. Burying her head in her hands, Natalie sobbed into her palms until they were soaked with her tears.

"Natalie? Are you all right?"

The voice at her side was unmistakably Evan's—she knew that without having to see his face. And he was the *last* person she wanted to see her cry but there he was, crouching beside her wearing an open expression of concern that only made her want to bawl that much harder.

"Go away," she said, crossing her arms across her drawn knees to bury her face in the crook of her elbow. "I'm fine."

"If you're fine then why are you crying?"

Natalie made an exasperated sound. *If I wanted to tell you that...*

She felt a hand gently caress the nape of her neck in a soothing gesture and her annoyance at his appearance melted. Lifting her head, she gave him an apologetic smile. "It's been a rough day."

Taking what she didn't say as an invitation to join her, Evan levered himself to her side, one arm resting on his bent knee. "Great view," he offered, surveying the landscape as Natalie had done before she started feeling sorry for herself.

Natalie nodded but kept silent.

"You know, Mrs. Stemming is going to be fine. Just in case you're still freaking out."

"I wasn't *freaking* out." Yes, she had and still was, but when he said it like that it made her feel like a ninny. She wiped away the last of her tears and her chin lifted a notch. "But even if I was…I don't believe a *little* freaking out would've been out of line. A. Woman. Fell. Out. Of. The. Boat."

Evan laughed, then immediately apologized. "You're right. It was fairly serious but everything worked out in the end. And, honestly, aside from the bruise, Mrs. Stemming thought it was a grand adventure."

"Yeah, well she's nuts," Natalie grumbled. The annoying urge to grin tugged at her lips until she had to make a deliberate effort to stop. Evan bumped her playfully with the side of his shoulder, earning a reciprocal one from her. This time she did smile and the mood lightened for a moment. An easy silence stretched between them until she turned to him, wondering why he was so calm when she was still reeling. "Weren't you scared? What if she'd died out there?" she asked.

Evan's smile faded and his gaze roamed her face as if committing it to memory, and a subtle shiver danced along her skin despite the heat of the afternoon.

"Has anyone ever told you you worry too much?" he asked, his voice a soft caress against her raw nerves.

Yes. "My sister, Nora," she admitted in a hoarse whisper, swallowing as she felt the short, yet respectable distance between them slowly close. Was he going to kiss her? For a wild disconcerting moment she desperately hoped so. Her heart thundered in her chest and her lips parted, whether in invitation or protest, she couldn't really be sure, but he smelled good enough to eat, which was patently ridiculous because he ought to have smelled like a dirty locker room after the day's exertion. But he didn't.

Seconds before the moment would've been right to end the torturous wondering of whether or not they should or shouldn't, the intense look in his eyes receded and the corner of his lips crooked as if in wry amusement as he pulled away, once again placing a respectable distance between them.

"Well, she's right. Mrs. Stemming is fine,

so stop worrying about what could've happened because it didn't."

Swimming in disappointment, she almost missed the gesture he made toward camp. "I've got to get back…." he said, rising from his crouched position. "If you're going to hang out a bit longer that's fine but I'd head back before it gets too dark. It's easy to twist an ankle out here."

"Thanks," she mumbled, still flustered by the fact that she'd wanted, no hungered, for his lips against hers. What kind of woman was she? One minute she was crying over Dan, and the next she was panting after a man she hardly knew. The soft crunching sound of Evan's shoes against the terrain receded and Natalie had to force herself not to take one last look. Gazing out toward the impressive landscape a sigh escaped that was equal parts wistful yearning and confused frustration as she tried sorting through the jumbled mess her mind had become.

Dan had her heart, didn't he?

Yes. Unequivocally.

Her eyes strayed from the beautiful vista and returned to the trail leading back to camp.

So, where did that leave room for Evan Murphy?

She compressed her lips and refused to answer, even in her head, but the question remained, dogging each step as she returned to camp.

Where, indeed?

CHAPTER SIX

THE NEXT TWO DAYS were smooth and as long as Evan kept a professional distance between him and Natalie, he was able to maintain his role of river guide—pleasant but not overly chatty—without wanting to grab her and jam his tongue down her throat. Just the errant thought, zinging through him with the force of a live wire, made him grimace. Scrubbing his palms over his face, he stopped long enough to check on Mrs. Stemming, who had made a miraculous recovery despite the ugly contusion on her knee, then made perfunctory checks with his crew to ensure everything was in order for dinner.

The sun was sinking fast and everyone was pretty tired. Today was the last day of rapids and they'd been pretty wild. A few times he thought Natalie was going to pass out, judging by the absence of blood in her cheeks, but she paddled as if her life had depended on it and a few times she'd even grinned. She had a great smile, he reflected absently, jerking when he realized what he was doing. *Dangerous territory, man.*

And she smelled good, too, a voice whispered as if his brain was at odds with…something else.

He shifted and was thankful for the denim shorts he'd chosen over his usual loose-fitting board shorts. She was hot, plain and simple. And that she didn't even know it was probably the kicker for him. Unlike Hailey, who'd known she was stunning and had often used it to her advantage. Her blond hair had been almost white, a color most people could only obtain through a bottle, but hers had been natural. And she had green eyes that put the brilliance of a gem to shame. Yeah, she'd been achingly beautiful, almost unreal, but the scars he carried were proof that she was no angel. More like a succubus. He shook off the memories, relieved they no longer left him feeling wretchedly empty.

Still, a pervading sense of "What the hell am I doing" dogged his consciousness and invaded his quiet moments. Natalie shared the same quality Hailey had used to twist his heart painfully around her finger: the sense that they were just wholesome, girl-next-door types. His mouth turned down in distaste as he mentally compared the two women. They weren't the same. He knew that…but a piece of him, a piece he'd buried a long time ago, struggled for the surface each time he looked at Natalie, reminding him of her and that made him uneasy.

The smell of dinner, tri-tip and roasted potatoes, made his mouth water and he pushed all thoughts of either woman from his mind. One more day and she'd be gone from his life. Something told him Natalie wasn't about to make river rafting her summer thing and he wasn't about to visit Emmett's Mill anytime soon. Their association with each other would end as abruptly as it started. And that was probably the best thing for everyone involved. He wasn't sure if his attraction was real or just some perverse desire to tease a part of his past to see if it still had the power to bite. Fortunately for them both, he had no intentions of testing that theory.

NATALIE CHEWED absently on her last mouthful of potato and allowed the heat from the fire to warm her chilled body. Mrs. Stemming had turned in early, only eating a few bites before yawning loudly and retiring. Her slight limp was the only sign the trip might be taking its toll on the older woman. Although she'd only just met her, Natalie was concerned about her and planned to approach Evan if she could ever get the man to stand still long enough to get a full sentence out.

Either he was avoiding her or she'd imagined their connection. If it was the first option, she could understand his reasons. There were probably rules against client/guide fraternization and they'd been *this* close to breaking them. But, if it was the second option, she didn't think her battered ego could take such a blow.

He walked into view and Natalie straightened, caught between the desire to confront him and the urge to run and hide. Paralyzed by her indecision, she remained, pulling the blanket around her tighter, yet tracking him surreptitiously with her eyes until she started to feel like some kind of weird stalker. Turning her attention away from Evan, she forced herself to find some interest in the conversation around the fire pit until the hour grew late and everyone sought their beds for the night.

She lingered at the fire, watching as the flames died to glowing embers, warding off the gathering chill in the air with their steady heat.

Little aches and pains blossomed in her muscles as she shifted in her foldout chair, a reminder that she wasn't in as good a shape as she'd thought, and wondered if Evan was in the same kind of discomfort. *Probably not.* He did this kind of thing all the time. The man was probably one solid mass of ripped muscle. A delicate shudder followed the silent musing and her toes curled inside her shoes.

"Not tired?"

Evan's voice beside her was startling. She turned sharply, watching as Evan rolled a chunk of wood from the woodpile beside her and sat down, her heart hammering loudly. She recovered enough to offer some sort of mumbled answer, but was too centered on the fact that she was incredibly pleased to have him there alone.

"I figured after today you'd be zonked. It

was pretty wild out there," he said, stretching his legs toward the dying fire and drawing her line of sight to the solid strength flexing beneath his worn hemp lounge pants. She jerked her gaze as her cheeks heated and was immediately thankful for the waning light. "What'd you think of the ride?" he asked, inclining his head to catch her answer, the vague curiosity in his stare overshadowed by something more intense that made the breath catch in her throat.

"There were a few times I thought we were going to die but you pulled us through," she admitted, as a small, almost playful smile threatened to blossom on her lips.

"Well, I try to keep my rafters alive—their word of mouth is better than the dead ones."

She cracked a wider smile. "I can imagine."

He was sitting so close she could catch a whiff of whatever he was wearing. He didn't seem the type to waste money on expensive cologne so she assumed it was just a combination of clean skin and rugged outdoors, but whatever it was she liked it. She leaned toward him to inhale another whiff. Her eyes fluttered shut for a brief moment as she savored whatever he was exuding, until his voice, low and curious, sounded in her ear.

"Natalie…?"

"Yeah?"

"What are you doing?"

She stared, wishing she had the where-withal to pull up and make some excuse, but she didn't so she answered honestly. "You smell good," she whispered. And look good. And probably taste good.

"Oh?"

She nodded, swallowing hard as his scent surrounded her. She lifted her gaze and he held it. "Evan?" she started, the husky tone of her voice barely above a murmur as a muscle flexed in his jaw.

"Yeah?" Dying firelight danced behind his eyes as he awaited her question. The intensity reflected back at her and trapped the air in her lungs until her breath was coming in short, tentative waves.

"Are you going to kiss me this time or not?"

HER QUESTION startled him but he doubted two seconds passed before he was in action. Before his brain had a chance to put up a good defense, his body was moving, grazing his lips against hers, eager to taste and impatient for more. Threading his fingers into the short soft waves on her head, he pushed his tongue into her mouth. When she responded eagerly, opening wider to accept him, he nearly wrenched her out of her chair in his desire to feel and touch more of her. "Natalie," he whispered against her lips, pausing in his sensual assault only long enough to offer some sort of warning, "this is a bad idea."

Her chest heaving, she agreed with a jerky movement of her head. "I know," she admitted in a breathy voice, her lips swollen and inviting, but she didn't seem ready to stop. A flicker of something wild and dangerous burst behind his sternum as he stood and pulled her to her feet with him. He drew her to him as he claimed her mouth again, their tongues meeting and tangling in a slick dance that heated his blood with the devastation of a forest fire. The heady rush of desire drowned the small, weak voice of caution advising him to keep his distance, and Evan gave in to the rippling pleasure. *So sweet.* He broke the kiss only long enough to travel to her neck, nipping at the sensitive skin until she gasped and clutched at his shoulders as her knees buckled.

"Are you sure?" he asked, trying one last time to hold onto some sense of propriety for both their sakes. When she answered by launching at his mouth with the same intensity, he nearly dragged her to his boat, his brain blanking as his body commanded his every movement. *This is right,* his body said as his hands roamed her body, impatient to feel her skin under his fingers.

No, it's not, a voice whispered in opposition.

Then, I don't care. He wasn't interested in listening to anything other than the sound of their labored breathing as they wrestled with their clothes, tearing at stubborn buttons— even popping one or two—until they were slipping under his blankets, skin on heated skin, oblivious to anything but their own need.

NATALIE CLOSED her eyes and sucked air between her teeth as Evan's hot mouth traveled a searing path down her quivering belly and settled for an intimate kiss pressed against the sensitive, barren skin of her pubic mound. A gasp escaped as he delved into her most private place, teasing her moist flesh until she twisted helplessly against every tantalizing sensation ricocheting through her body with the violence of a bullet as Evan coaxed her body into yielding the jackpot. Clenching her muscles against the waves of pleasure that radiated from the responsive nub, Natalie bit down on her knuckle to withhold the wild, gasping cry that threatened to erupt just as Evan appeared above her with a predatory grin and descended on her mouth. The smell of her own musk on his lips sent her tumbling over the edge, as he swallowed the second wave of sound breaking from her throat.

He made love to her mouth, plundering it with his tongue, deftly teasing until she was hot all over again, clutching at his shoulders and grinding against the hard ridge pressed against her thighs, until she was forced to demand in a guttural whisper, "Stop being such a tease, Evan!" for fear of dying from being denied that hot length a moment longer.

"Patience is a virtue," he said in a tight voice that changed to a soft groan as he paused to roll away and rummage impatiently through his bag. The sound of tearing foil followed and a feral grin curved her lips, so thankful for his foresight.

"Always prepared, I see," she said, inhaling sharply as he responded by descending on her exposed nipple, drawing hard enough to make her gasp but not enough to cause pain. Her head rocked from side to side as he laved each breast with his tongue, playing particular attention to the sensitive tips, until she was impatient for more.

"Now, Evan," she pleaded, pulling at his shoulders, the sound of his strained chuckle more effective than the most powerful aphrodisiac as she rose up to nip at the muscles cording his neck. "Now!"

He rewarded her fierce demand by gripping her hips and guiding himself into her, a groan escaping as he seated himself to the hilt. His eyes snapped open and a mixture of something she couldn't define reflected from his intense stare in the pale moonlight. Not wanting to know what lay behind that look, she squeezed her eyes shut and wrapped her legs around him, encouraging him to move hard and fast. She didn't want emotion. She wanted to drown in pleasure.

And, as Evan's hips rocked against hers and the telltale stirrings of another orgasm headed her way, she accepted everything Evan gave her with abandon. This was her moment and she wasn't going to waste it. The morning would come soon enough for them both.

CHAPTER SEVEN

EVAN'S HEART thundered in his throat as he lay beside Natalie, spent almost to the point of exhaustion, and stared at the stars, completely blown by the feelings that rocked him while having sex with Natalie.

"Please don't say you're sorry," she said, breaking into his thoughts with a hoarse whisper. He felt her head turn and he reluctantly met her steady gaze. Sweat-dampened hair clung to her crown and he had to resist the urge to smooth the errant curls from her forehead. A small smile followed as she said, "I'm not."

"You're not?"

"Not in the least," she answered, moonlight catching the gold chain around her neck, the pendant sliding to the side. She continued with a sigh. "I've been attracted to you since the first day. It was a relief to finally give in. Besides," she admitted in a low voice tinged with sadness, "it was good to feel something other than the pain of Dan's leaving and I'm going to bask in the moment at least for a little while."

"A little while?" he prompted, earning a wry but slightly playful smile in return.

"Well, of course," she answered as she turned to face him and slipped her arm beneath her head for a cushion. "I'll come to my senses eventually, but by that point, I'll be home and you'll be...wherever it is you go when you finish with these types of trips."

He went nowhere. Perhaps that was the problem. He offered a hollow chuckle to her watchful stare. "It's one gig after another. I raft all summer and teach skiing in the winter," he said, his voice low. "But they tend to blend after a while."

"I can imagine," she said, her tone faintly troubled.

Natalie absently reached for the pendant at her neck and he motioned toward the delicate jewelry. "What's that?"

"A gift from my older sister Tasha. When I touch it, somehow it makes me feel brave even when I'm scared out of my mind."

"Are you scared right now?" he asked.

Natalie met his gaze. "No."

"I'm glad."

He smiled softly as he traced a finger down the curve of her jaw in a motion that was almost subconscious. "What happens when you go home? What's waiting for you there?"

Natalie paused as if wondering the same and a subtle frown pulled at her brows before she broke the reflective silence with her answer. "Well, my job is waiting for me."

"And what do you do?"

"Nothing exciting, believe me. My life is pretty sedate." She pursed her lips, muttering almost to herself. "At least to hear Dan tell it, that is."

Dan again. Evan didn't know this Dan character but already he didn't think much of him. The man was obviously an idiot and she was probably better off without the jackass. He pulled her closer and she snuggled into his body as if she were made to fit. "And what is this sedate life?" he asked, resisting the urge to start all over again.

She chuckled. "The life of a librarian."

"You're nothing like the librarians I used to know," he murmured, earning another soft-throated laugh. "You're way hotter."

"Oh? And how many librarians have you known in your life?"

"Two."

"Two?"

"Yes," he continued, pausing long enough to nuzzle the sweet-smelling skin of her neck. "Mrs. Brioske and Mr. Halibut."

"And?"

"And neither one were what anyone could confuse with 'hot.'" He turned her onto her back, privately enjoying the way the moonlight caressed her fair skin and shimmered in her hair. "Mrs. Brioske was grouchy with a habit of passing out detention slips to anyone who didn't share her love for books, and Mr. Halibut was too old to do anything but sleep behind the counter."

"Well, I'm glad to hear I've changed your opinion on librarians," she said, closing her eyes. An incredible sense of intimacy surrounded them and Evan was greedy to know more about the woman nestled beside him. Her eyes fluttered open and a moment passed between them that was full of wonder and discovery. "What are you thinking?" she ventured, a subtle wariness entering her gaze.

He shook his head, unwilling to share the unfamiliar feelings curling inside him. Instead, his mouth crooked and he changed the subject. "So, if being a librarian is so sedate...then switch it up. Try something different."

"Oh, yeah? Like what?" she countered playfully. "Something like river-rafting?"

"Something like that," he said, chuckling and trailing his finger down her jaw to the valley between her breasts. He stopped to press a lingering kiss on the smooth flesh. He smiled at her reaction, enjoying the way her body reacted to his touch. "What's your dream? Why not start there?"

She sighed. "My dream."

"What is it?" he asked, encouraged by her wistful expression. He nudged her when she hesitated. "Come on. You can tell me. I promise it can't be anything crazier than what I've been doing the past ten years."

Bolstered, she started, "Well...I always dreamed of opening a children's bookstore. Something small and cozy with little reading areas filled with beanbag chairs and fuzzy throw rugs that were just right for snuggling up with a good book."

"That doesn't sound so crazy," he responded encouragingly and her smile widened as she continued.

"And I'd have story hours for the little ones and an education section filled with the classics, such as Hawthorne, Twain and the Brontë sisters for older readers needing a copy for their lessons at school. I'd fill that place so full of books that you wouldn't be able to find a flat surface without a stack of them."

Her enthusiasm was infectious and he was easily swept up in the moment, smiling as he asked, "So, what is this amazing bookstore called?"

She gave a sheepish grin and her shoulder lifted in a shrug. "I don't know. Haven't thought that far yet."

"Why not? It sounds like a great idea but you need a name."

"No, it's just wishful thinking. I don't know the first thing about owning a business. Besides, my dad said a niche market like that would go belly up in the first year. And I don't have the extra cash lying around to just throw down the toilet."

"What about a small business loan?" he suggested, not quite ready to let the conversation end, despite the niggling voice that had started to warn him to back off.

"A business loan?"

"Sure," he answered, ignoring his gut instinct. "If you've got good enough credit and the lender is satisfied with your business plan, you could secure a loan to get things started."

"How do you know so much about business?" she asked, regarding him curiously.

"I—" *have a master's degree in the subject,* he almost said but somehow managed to bite it back and finish with something noncommittal. "I have friends who know a bit about business and I pay attention."

"Oh," she answered, her lips twisting into a playful smile as she wound her arms around his neck. "What else do you know? About business…"

"I know…that some of the best small businesses cater to niche markets," he answered in a throaty whisper, his blood heating as she pressed her lithe frame against all the right spots. "And…" He groaned as she slipped her hand beneath the blanket that covered them to lightly palm the twins, almost eclipsing his ability to think clearly. With almost superhuman effort he pulled the hand lightly caressing his sensitive skin and cradled it in his, curling in toward his chest. "I think if you want to open a business…you should."

She sighed softly, the sound pulling at his heart strongly enough to make him frown. "Well, I'll probably just stick to where I'm at. It's a good place. Stable and steady."

"Stable is good but if owning a children's bookstore is your dream, you should go for it. Take a chance, Natalie. You might just like it."

She looked at him sharply and the vulnerable quality returned to her gaze. "Evan, I'm not good at taking chances—that's why Dan left."

"Dan left because he's an idiot," he muttered darkly, sealing his lips to hers and swallowing her surprised gasp. Her mouth opened, silently offering more, and he gladly took it, deepening the kiss until they were both shaking with the need raging between them. He wanted her again—now. But he pulled himself back, knowing somehow that if he didn't stop, there'd be no turning back and neither of them was ready for whatever that could mean. Rolling away, it was a long moment before either spoke again, and Evan cursed silently for saying anything about her ex-boyfriend. It hadn't been his place, but knowing how much she was hurting inside over that jackass made him want to go find the guy and punch his lights out. As the desire ebbed from his veins, reality came creeping back and he knew somehow he'd allowed himself to cross the line he'd always given ample berth.

Turning, he found her watching him. He drew a deep breath, but as he started to speak she shushed him with a finger to his lips.

"Let's not ruin it, okay?"

He was tempted to kiss the sensitive pad but controlled the impulse. When she withdrew her finger he made no move to stop her. Something close to disappointment flashed in her eyes but it was gone in the next instant as she searched the boat for her discarded clothing. Seconds later, she had pulled her shirt over her head, the fabric concealing from view her gorgeous breasts that had fit perfectly in his palms as if they'd been made exclusively for him. It was smart to let her go back to her tent, to pretend none of this had happened, but Evan was struggling with what his brain was telling him. She made a move to grab her other clothing and Evan snaked an arm out and curled it around her waist, drawing her against him.

"Stay," he said gruffly, rubbing his chin against the nape of her neck as she softened into the curve of his frame, her behind fitting nicely into the cove created by his hips. The immediate heat of their bodies felt like a warm embrace and he smiled when she relaxed into his hold.

His last thought before dropping into a contented slumber was that sleeping with Natalie was the most natural feeling in the world—too bad it couldn't last.

CHAPTER EIGHT

EIGHT WEEKS LATER Natalie stared at the small indicator window and worried her bottom lip. Not a double pink line, please, she begged, gripping the rubber handle so tight it shook in her hand.

Please, only one line!

Natalie's head fell into her hands and a mournful sound escaped that would've been pitifully embarrassing if she hadn't been alone. She lifted her head and checked her watch.

It was time—yet instead of snatching the stick with shaking fingers, her gaze bounced away from the indicator window almost involuntarily.

"Just get it over with," she muttered. It was probably just a slight hormonal glitch in her system. After all the stress she'd been going through lately with the opening of her bookstore it would hardly be surprising. Besides, her periods had never been normal anyway.

A few more similar statements later she'd almost convinced herself the opposite of what she knew in her heart—until her eyes found the window and her whole world froze with the discovery.

She was pregnant.

"Pregnant," she gasped, the word penetrating her stunned brain with painful precision. *Oh, Evan.* His name came out with another guttural moan. There was no doubt; he'd been the only one since Dan had left months prior. How could she be so stupid? So *irresponsible?* The last word she heard through her father's voice and cringed. They'd used protection, she was sure of it, but the proof that something had gone wrong was staring her right in the face. Why now? Of all the bad timing!

She continued to stare at the offending stick, desperately hoping she'd perhaps read the test wrong, when the front door opened and she nearly fell into the bathtub.

"Just me," Nora called out as Natalie sprang into horrified action, trying to hide the evidence of her situation from her sister's all-too sharp attention. "Where are you?"

Natalie shoved the test box and the contents into the empty wastebasket beside the toilet and tried crumpling a swath of toilet paper to stick on top before Nora rounded the short corner and realized she was trying to hide something. "Just…a minute," she stammered, unable to quell the panic in her voice.

"What's wrong?" Nora appeared by the doorway just as Natalie slammed the bathroom door shut behind her, her pert features instantly on alert. "You're pale and…a little greasy. Are you sick?"

So much for that pregnant glow. Natalie made her way past her sister with a shaky laugh. "Greasy? Thanks. It's called sweat. Haven't you noticed it's about four hundred degrees in here?"

It was hot. Larry, the apartment manager, had conveniently forgotten to return her message about the broken air-conditioning and it was sweltering outside. If it weren't for her floor fans, she might've died of heat exhaustion long ago.

"Aren't they required by law to fix stuff like that?" Nora's nose crinkled even as she pulled her blond hair into a messy ponytail at the base of her neck.

"I suppose."

"Are you sure you're okay?" Nora gave her a hard stare. "You really don't look good."

"I'm fine." She wasn't sure what she was going to do but she knew she wasn't ready to share. Forcing a bright smile, she headed for the kitchen for something cool to drink. "What brings you by?"

"I got a postcard from Tasha, thought you might like to read it," Nora answered, reaching behind her to pull it from the back pocket of her jean shorts. But just as Natalie reached for it, Nora jerked it out of reach. "Not until you tell me what's wrong."

Not on your life. *"Nothing,"* she said, adding a hint of exasperation to her tone. "Will you let it go already? I'm hot, tired and…that's all. Now, let me see the postcard. Where is she these days?"

"Belize again," came Nora's short answer as she reluctantly handed over the card, her expression changing. "Thank God she's not in Uganda anymore. Did you know volunteers get abducted all the time and used as political pawns or worse? Knowing Tasha, she'd be the first to get snatched if things went sour. It drives me nuts that she renewed another three-year term."

"Well, it's important to her," Natalie answered, distracted by the all-too short correspondence. She'd harbored much of the same feelings when Tasha had abruptly announced during her last year of college, much to the outright shock and sputtering disapproval of their father, that she was dropping out to join the Peace Corps. Natalie flipped the card, the front featuring the ruins of a Mayan village, and reread the back, wishing there was more.

"So, how's the shop coming? You reach the last layer of wallpaper yet?"

Natalie returned the postcard and exhaled loudly, shaking her head in frustration. "I'm on the third layer. I figure eventually I'll either hit the original wall or I'll fall through to the alley, but I'm not stopping until I do."

"Sounds like a plan. Need any help? I've got a few free days between projects."

"Absolutely," Natalie answered, relieved to have some help since neither of her parents had been entirely supportive of her decision to quit her job at the library to open her own business, The Dragon's Lair. The news of her unexpected pregnancy was likely to send them over the edge.

She had a difficult time swallowing and covered with a hasty sip of her lemonade, which had warmed in her hand, the sour taste almost making her gag.

"So, are you coming to dinner tonight?"

The thought of food made her instantly queasy but she nodded. "I'm bringing the pasta salad Dad likes, the one with the artichoke hearts and red peppers." She looked at Nora. "Why? Aren't you?"

Nora's shrug was noncommittal. "I don't know. I'm really not in the mood to argue with Dad all night. I'm sure the conversation will inevitably turn to Tasha and I don't want to hear it."

"So, don't argue with him," Natalie countered, to which she earned a derisive look. "He just wants to feel validated. You know his blustering is just a front. He worries about her."

"Concerned fathers don't refuse to talk to their daughters, no matter how wayward."

What would her dad think when he found out she was pregnant? By a man she hardly even knew? She avoided Nora's stare, afraid her sister would see the sudden shine in her eyes as her bottom lip threatened to quiver and shatter the facade she was desperately trying to hold onto. "Well, it's the only way he knows how to deal with his feelings," she said briskly, drawing a deep breath and searching wildly for neutral territory. "How's business?"

"Oh, fine," Nora answered, a subtle glower still lingering in her expression. "It was slow during the winter but that's to be expected. Not many people are thinking about their yards when it's raining outside."

Nora was a landscape architect, something her father predicted would never work out in a town as small as theirs. But she'd proven him wrong and was actually thriving. Nora's success gave her hope that her own venture would find solid ground. That, combined with Evan's belief that she could do it, had helped give her the confidence to put together a business plan and approach the local bank for a SBA loan. "Good for you. I knew you'd do great. You're a natural with anything green. Unlike me, who can't seem to keep my one plant from looking as if it's one step away from death every day."

"It can't be that bad," Nora said with a laugh, sobering long enough to offer some green-thumb tips. "The trick is to water in the morning, not at night so the roots aren't sitting in water…."

Natalie nodded as Nora went on but her mind was elsewhere. Where did Evan fit into this picture? She had to tell him. Didn't she? Of course she did. He was the father. He deserved to know. What if he didn't want to be a father? This was a hell of a thing to spring on a guy without any warning. She had nine months to figure out a way to break it to him. Somehow…that didn't seem like enough time.

Nora, realizing Natalie had drifted yet again, put her hands on her hips and demanded her attention. "Listen, something's going on with you and I'm not leaving until you tell me what it is."

The protests that readily jumped to her tongue died in the face of Nora's determined expression. Nora was nothing if not stubborn and she'd badger Natalie until she uncovered the truth.

Still, Natalie wished her brain was working better so she could find a way to convince her baby sister all was well. But somehow the words came to her lips and then fell out of her mouth in a strangled whisper and there was nothing she could do to take them back.

"I'm pregnant."

Nora gasped and her eyes widened until they looked like big, gray marbles that might just plop right out of her sockets and roll around on the floor. "You're *what?*"

"Pregnant."

"What…" Nora stopped, momentarily speechless for perhaps the first time in her life, and gave her head a shake, still reeling. "What are you going to do?"

A sad smile lifted the corner of her mouth. "I haven't a clue."

Nora's mouth worked as if she wasn't sure where to start and the ensuing chaos in her brain was short-circuiting her motor skills. "Who's the father?" she finally managed to ask, then gasped again, this time the sound more horrified than shocked. "Please don't tell me it's Dan's baby!"

A mild spasm reminded Natalie of her previous heartache but it wasn't nearly as bad as she thought it would be. She shook her head and Nora's expression went from relieved, which was slightly annoying, to puzzled. "Who then?"

"What difference does it make? Knowing the father's identity isn't going to change anything." Natalie set her glass down and pulled her hair away from the nape of her neck, closing her eyes in relief as the fan cooled her skin. God, it was hot. She opened her eyes again and sighed. "You don't know him, okay?"

"Oh my God…you hooked up with someone on your rafting trip!"

Natalie winced, thinking that statement couldn't have sounded sluttier, and wondered if she should've made something up. Of course, she was a terrible liar so Nora would've sniffed out the truth eventually, but maybe she'd have had time to adjust to the idea. Hindsight was always 20/20, as they said. Still, Nora's comment felt like a poke in the eye and she reacted. "You're one to talk! You slept with your first client and I never freaked out on you."

"Totally different and you know it," Nora returned, pink crawling into her cheeks as she lifted her chin. "We used to date in high school. And I didn't get pregnant!"

"Details," she grumbled, waving away Nora's outrage. Why hadn't she kept her ever-blooming mouth shut? It was going to be hard enough to deal with her father much less her younger sister, who never knew when to leave well enough alone. "Yes, I met someone on the trip but…it wasn't like we were planning to ever see each other again, you know? And quit looking at me like that—I already feel rotten…and queasy to boot."

"Is he…decent?" At Natalie's sharp look, she rushed to clarify. "What I mean is…will he step up or will he bail as soon as he finds out?"

Natalie blocked out the image of Evan as a father. She wasn't ready. She needed more time. "I don't know what he'll do. I'm trying not to think about it. Besides, I'm not sure it's smart to tie myself to a man who makes his living rafting and skiing as if life is just one big party." At Nora's gathering frown, Natalie continued, ignoring her sister's expression. "I was in an emotionally vulnerable place, Nora. You know, if I'd been thinking straight I wouldn't have slept with someone who's practically a stranger. It's not now, nor has it ever been, my style."

"Neither is river-rafting, but hey, you're the one trying new things," Nora quipped, earning a glare from Natalie. "Right. Not helpful. So, when are you going to tell him?"

"I'm not sure…definitely not tonight," she answered, distress pulling at her brows. "I need more time to—"

"Not our dad, you dope," Nora cut in. "The *baby's* dad."

"Oh." Natalie's shoulders slumped in relief. "How about never?"

"What?"

Nora's screech and ensuing expression of disbelief reinforced Natalie's previous wish that she'd kept her mouth shut. Nora would never understand a decision like that. She was, for all her independence, a hopeless romantic. Natalie didn't have the luxury of dreaming about happy endings involving total strangers. As much as she might wish it, she was not starring in her own version of a Sandra Bullock movie about fated love. The facts were distressingly blunt and no fairy-tale in sight—she was single and pregnant.

"I didn't ask for this, Nora," Natalie answered, her voice cool despite the unpredictable state of her emotions as of late. "And neither did Evan." At the mention of his name, she almost slapped a palm to her forehead. Why couldn't she keep her damned mouth shut? Now Nora had a name with which to badger her. She drew a deep breath. Perhaps she'd completely gloss over that small detail.

"Evan…Evan who?"

"Never mind. It doesn't matter. The fact is I haven't decided what I'm going to do and I don't need the added complication."

"He has rights, too, Natalie."

"Not if he doesn't know."

The silence between them lengthened and Nora seemed to grudgingly agree, but before Natalie could steer the conversation in a different direction she returned with renewed curiosity.

"How'd this happen?"

Natalie arched her brow as if to say *the usual way* and Nora clarified.

"You're, as Dad *so* likes to put it, the responsible one. I mean, nobody's perfect but you come pretty damn close. I just can't imagine you doing something so out of character. A fling with a total stranger is not your M.O."

"Thanks for pointing out the obvious," she

grumbled, as a tear slipped from the corner of her eye.

"So what changed?" Nora reached up and wiped the tear away, the action tender though her expression was troubled.

"I told you I was vulnerable and Evan was…" Sweet, charming—all the things Dan had not been as he'd crushed her hopes and dreams with one wretched sentence before walking out of her life. "Available. He'd been available. He's no one special. I don't know him from Adam, Nora. How do I know what kind of father he'll be? He could be a total pig for that matter. Forgive me if I want a little time to think this through. I'd rather just leave him out of the equation. What's so hard to understand?"

"Well, when you put it like that…" Nora said, not the least bit apologetic for her opinion, nor entirely convinced by Natalie's outburst. She groaned, then added, "I'm sorry but being responsible is in your marrow, probably even etched into your DNA, and even though this was something out of character, I don't think your internal monitors would lead you so far afield from your moral compass. I'm willing to bet this guy's not the Lothario you're so willing to paint him to be."

A twinge of guilt flashed through her. Evan wasn't a bad guy. Far from it. "He wasn't bad," she heard herself say. "He was amazing."

But there was no sense in compounding the problem. Evan was the least of her worries. He didn't know and for now, that was a good thing. It gave her time to think of a way to break it to him.

EVAN MURPHY dragged one eye open and instantly closed it again as the sunlight from the open window assaulted his corneas with a vengeance.

Hell, John. He grumbled and turned his head away from the open window, cursing his older brother and pulling the pillow over his head. He'd taken the red-eye out of Utah so he could help Paul Houston, the owner of Wild River Expeditions, secure the J-rig and paddleboat in the storage facility before he went home. He'd only gotten a few hours' sleep. Over the past few years the quality of Paul's employees had disintegrated, leaving him to do all the cleanup once the gig was done. He hated to leave the old guy in the lurch so he always hung around after everyone else had already taken off, ready to spend the cash Paul gave them under the table. But usually that meant he was left to catch the latest flight and, lately, his body didn't quite bounce back as easily as it used to when he was twenty-five.

Sliding on a pair of jeans, he padded into the kitchen with a yawn, searching out a source of caffeine to jolt his sleeping senses awake.

Grabbing a chipped mug from the cabinet he poured himself a steaming cup and watched his older brother from the kitchen window directly above the old porcelain sink. John had turned the ranch their parents had owned, before their dad split, into a successful business boarding horses, but his real gift was working with the ones that were skittish or injured. Evan liked to tease his older brother, calling him the Horse Whisperer of Mariposa County, but for all his ribbing he couldn't deny his brother had talent.

Squinting into the bright morning sun, Evan joined his brother with mug in hand at the small arena as John walked a chestnut quarter horse.

"Sleep good?"

Evan allowed a smile in spite of his earlier annoyance. "Would've been better if someone hadn't opened the blinds at the crack of dawn."

The corner of John's mouth twitched but he returned his attention to the horse, seeming to study its gait. "How was Utah?"

"Good."

"You going back?"

Evan took a sip. "Doubt it. I was just filling in while Paul was shorthanded. Besides, I've got a few short gigs coming up here in California to keep me busy until the end of the season."

Since he lived with his brother, it was enough money to put away in savings and live off until the next gig. In the meantime, he helped his brother out around the ranch, though after a month or two of shoveling horse crap he was ready to do something else. Ranch life didn't hold the same appeal to Evan as it did for John—frankly, it was too close to what their father had tried and failed at for Evan to completely embrace.

"When you going to put that fancy degree of yours to good use?"

"I like what I do." Evan's mouth tightened

as irritation washed over him. "I make a decent living."

"Just seems like a waste having that piece of paper and nothing to show for it."

Evan pushed away from the wooden fence. "John, I just got back and I'm not even awake yet. I paid you back so don't worry about how I put my education to use. All right? Just leave it."

The chestnut, sensing the tension, tossed his head and nickered as if to say "take it on the road," and Evan obliged. "Good to see you, John."

Right.

Good mood evaporating, Evan returned to the house and went to his room to unpack, though he'd rather pick up and go again. Each time he came home it was the same conversation. Somehow John thought since he helped put Evan through college he had some say in his life. Well, that may have been true before he paid back his debt, but he was free and clear of that obligation.

He was beholden to no one—and that was just the way he liked it.

CHAPTER NINE

NORA STUCK a cherry tomato in her mouth before she said something she'd regret later as her father continued on his usual tirade at dinner.

"It's damned ridiculous if you ask me," Gerald Simmons grumbled before stabbing a generous piece of steak and jamming it in his mouth. Unfortunately, Nora noted, the meat wasn't big enough to keep his blessed trap shut for a second. "That's no life for a woman. Belize? What's Belize got that we don't have right here?"

"The jungle," Nora quipped under her breath and Gerald looked at her sharply.

"How's business coming?" Missy Simmons interjected quickly, her light blue eyes wide as she made an effort to keep the peace between them. "I just saw Mrs. Crabbins's yard yesterday and it's absolutely stunning." She turned to Gerald, her gaze pleading. "Didn't I say Mrs. Crabbins's yard was beautiful?" When Gerald acknowledged the comment with a grunt and her mother just smiled, Nora wanted to shake her. "So, do you have any big projects?"

Actually, she did but she had no interest in sharing her exciting news around her father. She'd recently landed a major client—a bed-and-breakfast—and they wanted to overhaul the entire landscape from desert palms to manicured Japanese gardens. A smile started to grow in anticipation of the job, but she quelled the impulse, managing a minor shrug. "Nothing special. Just a few backyards here and there. You know, the usual."

"I thought you said business was good?" Although phrased as a question, it came out sounding accusatory and Nora was about ready to pitch the bread she was idly toying with at his head. The only reason she'd agreed to come along in the first place was because Natalie had practically begged her.

"Daddy, Nora is the best landscape architect from here to Coldwater," Natalie said, surprising Nora with her defense. Natalie flicked her gaze to her as if to say thanks for enduring what was turning out to be an excursion into obligatory hell and continued, "In fact, she has a waiting list a year long. You don't get that sought after if you're not good at what you do."

"Well, that's a fact," he said, his voice losing some of its edge until he changed directions, eyeing Natalie with a frown. "So have you come to your senses yet and gone back to the library before you lose everything in this foolhardy venture you call a bookstore?"

"Dad, don't be like that. The bookstore is not foolhardy. Some of the most successful businesses cater to niche markets. Don't worry, I've done my homework. Besides," Natalie continued, drawing a deep breath and braving a bright smile that even to Nora looked forced, "it's coming along fabulously. You should come by and see it when I have it all finished. Right now, I'm tearing down old wallpaper."

"I've always wondered what the old Galupi building looked like inside," Missy said. "It's probably at least a hundred years old. What do you think, Gerald?"

"What are you doing for money?" he

asked, bypassing both Natalie's offer and Missy's question.

"I told you," Natalie answered, pushing her plate aside and meeting their father's hard stare. "I qualified for a good-sized SBA loan." When he didn't seem satisfied with her answer, she added, "And Marilyn said they could always use a little part-time help down at the library if things get a bit tight before the shop opens."

Nora wondered if that was true but resisted shooting her sister a questioning glance. Another forced smile fitted itself to her sister's lips and Nora had her answer.

"I'll be fine, Daddy," Natalie offered to their father's silent assessment. "Really."

"Well, if you say so, we believe you," Missy said, sending a quick smile Natalie's way. "You've always had a good head on your shoulders."

"True enough," Gerald conceded, returning to his dinner. "Those pictures of Utah were real good," he said, gesturing to Natalie with his fork. "Reminds me of when your mom and me took that trip into the Grand Canyon years ago."

"When was that?" Nora couldn't contain

the surprise or cynicism from her voice. Her father? On a vacation? She'd never seen it, so Nora had a hard time believing it. As a former battalion chief for the California Department of Forestry, their father had been a workaholic of the first order.

"Before Tasha was born," her mother interjected softly, her eyes darting to Nora as if silently pleading for her to tread cautiously around the subject of their sister. Nora bit her tongue for her mother's sake. "It was quite lovely, though. We really enjoyed ourselves. Biking, kayaking—we did it all. Fun stuff."

"Never did go rafting, though," Gerald added, his tone vaguely regretful. He returned his attention to Natalie. "What was it like?"

Natalie stopped fidgeting with her napkin and offered a tight smile. "You know me, Dad. Not really the adventurous type. It wasn't my cup of tea. It was actually pretty frightening at times. I don't think I will ever do it again."

"Well, I'm glad you tried it at least," he said, his voice softening, and Nora felt an odd pang of jealousy that immediately shamed her. She exchanged a private look with Natalie, who seemed ready to break under the strain of her secret, and felt even worse. While their father always seemed to find fault with her, Natalie had always been his golden girl. But with his admiration came a certain pressure that Nora was glad she didn't have to bear.

By night's end Nora's exhaustion mirrored the fatigue bracketing her sister's eyes.

"You okay?" she asked as they walked to their cars.

"Tired."

"I'll bet. When are you going to see a doctor?"

Natalie gave an unhappy little sigh and shot Nora a look.

"What?"

"I don't really want to talk about it. Besides, if I go to someone in town word will spread before I'm even done with the exam. I need to deal with this in my own time. I don't need people hovering over me."

Even you, her look communicated, but Nora knew her sister. She had a tendency to bury her head in the sand in the hopes that whatever was bothering her would eventually go away.

"Don't wait too long. You're already… what, almost two months, possibly more? There's all sorts of bloodwork you have to get done and—"

"Nora!" Natalie said, the force of her name coming out in an exasperated gasp. "I *know* what needs to be done. I only just found out, okay? I need some time to get used to the idea."

"Right. Sorry," she answered, truly apologetic. The last thing she wanted to do was push Natalie away, but it didn't sit right that she wanted to exclude the father. If he wasn't a bad guy and he might even want to be a father, didn't she owe it to him to at least tell him? "Do you need anything?"

"Just sleep." Natalie drew a deep breath and opened her car door. "Thanks for not spilling the beans to Dad. I know he was probably standing on your last nerve—"

"More like jumping on it," she cut in wryly.

"Well…thanks for keeping my secret."

Nora gave a short nod and watched as Natalie climbed into her Honda Civic. As she turned to get into her own car, Natalie's voice made her turn.

"You know he doesn't mean to hurt your feelings when he says stuff like that…."

Nora ground her teeth. Why did she always defend him? "Yes, he does."

"It's just his way of showing he cares."

"Natalie…don't. We don't have the same relationship so don't even try to draw parallels."

"Sometimes Dad doesn't realize—"

"Nat, I hate to shatter whatever illusions you have about our father but things are going to change once you tell him your little secret," Nora interrupted, her blunt statement causing Natalie to draw back as if she'd just been slapped. The sudden glitter in her eyes made Nora feel like a jerk but she couldn't take it back because she was afraid it was true. The only reason their father favored Natalie was because she was a pushover, just like their mom. Nora reached out toward her sister but she'd already disappeared into the dark interior of the car.

"I'll call you later," she called out, the sick, awful feeling of guilt almost cutting off her ability to speak coherently.

Natalie offered a wave to indicate she'd heard her but within minutes she was driving away, leaving Nora to curse herself for being so insensitive. Maybe Natalie was right—she and her dad were more alike than she liked to admit.

EVAN LIFTED his oversized duffel bag and gave it a shake to dislodge any dirt or pebbles he'd inadvertently added to his luggage during the trip, when something shiny tumbled with a barely discernable sound to the porch.

Puzzled, he bent to retrieve it, immediately recognizing the white-gold chain as memories of one moonlit night tumbled through his brain. Running the callused pad of his thumb over the sapphire stone that floated in the center of a small heart, he was conflicted by the feelings that sprang to life by the remembrance.

Careful not to damage it, he coiled the necklace in his palm and carried it into the house.

Natalie.

Even without the necklace she hadn't been far from his thoughts. In his younger days, part of the allure of being a river guide was the idea of hot women in bikinis looking for adventure, but he was long past his promiscuous days of one-night stands.

And that thought made the night with Natalie stand out all the more.

He shook his head, rubbing the scruff on his chin wistfully, and allowed the memories to wash over him like a soft caress.

What to do…

Staring at the necklace, he was caught in a foreign position. He made a point not to get involved with the women he met working the river or the slopes. Usually he made sure there was an understanding between them before anything progressed beyond playful flirting.

But he hadn't given Natalie his practiced speech about how he wasn't the type to settle down before taking things to the next level. No, he thought, frowning, he'd been too blinded by his overwhelming desire to get to know her. Something about her had tugged hard and he'd given little resistance.

And she was still on his mind. Bad sign. It wasn't often he gave much more thought to the temporary interludes he enjoyed now and then after the final goodbyes were said. But here he sat, reminiscing about a woman he'd only known six days, replaying their short time together in his head as if it were his favorite movie and he had the best seats in the house. He chuckled, the sound echoing his uncertain mood, and he wondered how to categorize the allure of Natalie Simmons.

Sure, she'd been sweet—in a wounded and breakable sort of way—but Evan didn't harbor any illusions about being the knight in shining armor.

He eyed the necklace. By now she's realized it was missing, he thought. Probably figured it was long gone. It wouldn't take much to track her down, he mused, surprising himself when he actually gave it thought instead of shooting the idea down immediately.

What did he look like? The lost-and-found?

"Evan, you coming or what?" John's voice called from outside his window. "Time's a wastin'."

"Be right there," he hollered back, resolving to deal with the necklace issue later. It wasn't as if it was going anywhere.

That night, stinking and dirty from helping John mend a fence in the back field, he pulled his shirt over his head and mopped the sweat from his face before tossing it in the dirty clothes hamper. A dip in the crisp waters of a river would be heaven right about now, he thought as he settled for a cool shower.

As the water sluiced over the top of him, he closed his eyes and tried to keep his mind blank, to enjoy the simple pleasure of cool water on his heated skin. Unbidden thoughts of Natalie surfaced and he wondered if he was suffering from some kind of karmic backlash for past transgressions. Shutting off the water, the old pipes rattling as the pressure receded, he stepped from the shower and wrapped a towel around his mid-section.

Ruffling the water from his hair with his hand, he walked to his dresser, where a small address book sat on top of loose change he'd pulled from his jeans last night before he'd fallen into bed. Thumbing to the section with Paul's phone number, he punched the number into his cell phone.

"Hey, Paul?" he said when the older man answered, closing the book and sitting on the edge of his bed. "Yeah, Evan here. Say, I've got some personal property left behind by one of the rafters. Think I could ship it to you and you could return it?"

"Evan, you know I don't do that. It's part

of the paperwork they sign. Wild River Expeditions is not responsible for lost valuables. It says right there in the fine print."

Evan smiled. He'd always thought it was ironic that Paul was paranoid about being sued yet didn't harbor a healthy fear of the IRS when he paid his employees under the table. "Listen, man, I know what the paperwork says…I helped draft it for you, remember? It's just a necklace but I got the impression it was pretty special to her. I'm sure she'd like it back."

"Who's the owner?" he asked, mildly curious in spite of his stand on the issue.

"You probably wouldn't remember her… tall girl with short, dark blond hair…uh, Natalie Simmons was her name."

Paul made a whistling sound. "Oh, I remember her all right. Pretty girl."

"And young enough to be your granddaughter," Evan retorted, immediately grossed out by the image of his hippie friend leering at Natalie in a way that was less than neighborly. "Can you return it to her? You should have her mailing address on her paperwork."

"Sorry, no can do, brother. Rules are rules, you know."

Evan frowned, biting his tongue just as he started to remind Paul that he was never one to live by the letter of the law. Why start now with one small policy? "All right, the rules don't say anything about me returning the necklace personally so just give me her address and I'll mail it to her."

There was a pause as Paul considered Evan's offer. "What about confidentiality and all that stuff?"

"You can trust me. I just want to return the damn necklace, not stalk the woman."

"All right but if she finds out and presses charges, you're on your own, brother."

"Fine." He sighed, waiting for the address.

He hung up and wrestled with the temptation that was pulling him in a direction that only promised trouble. *Slip it in the mail*, a voice warned when he pictured taking the drive to return it in person. Natalie's face popped into his mind as he gently jostled the necklace in his palm. Emmett's Mill was only an hour away.... Where was the harm in seeing her one last time? As far as he knew they'd parted amicably. He grinned at the prospect, ignoring the warning buzz still sounding at the back of his skull. What if she wanted to pick up where they left off? His smile faltered as he carefully returned the necklace to his dresser. What if she considered his visit an invitation for more?

Stop being so paranoid.

He was just being neighborly.

He'd drop it off, perhaps chat for a while, and they'd part ways.

No strings. No problem.

His smile returned. He'd leave first thing in the morning.

CHAPTER TEN

NATALIE EMERGED from the bathroom, one hand clutching her stomach and the other wiping the sweat from her forehead as Nora cast a sympathetic look her way.

"That bad, huh?"

"It's a wonder the human race has survived this long," Natalie answered, collapsing on the sofa beside Nora with a groan. "I can't keep anything down."

"You really should see a doctor."

"I will."

"When?"

Natalie sighed. "When I don't have a million and one other things to think about." Nora's expression darkened and Natalie could almost hear the dialogue running through her brain. "I *will* see the doctor, Nora. I promise. I'm barely ten weeks. I have some time yet so stop worrying."

"I'd stop worrying if you'd stop being so pigheaded and go and see a doctor now." Nora picked up a magazine to fan herself. "And when is the manager going to fix the air conditioner in this place? You're in a delicate freaking position, for crying out loud."

The heat was oppressive even for late August but Natalie couldn't deal with Larry right now. She had to figure out what she was going to do about her shop. The work wasn't going to finish itself and her deadline was fast approaching. She didn't have long before her grand opening was scheduled and thus far, all she had to show for it were antique wallpaper hanging limply off the walls and iffy plumbing. Unfortunately, she'd been unable to stray far from the toilet; certain smells, particularly old wallpaper, made her stomach rebel.

The building had been a steal, but as Natalie got further into remodelling she realized why the lease had been so accommodating. She clapped a hand over her eyes and groaned as another wave of nausea rolled through her.

She didn't know the first thing about pregnancy but she'd read morning sickness usually only lasted through the first trimester, so if she could tough it out for a few more weeks, at least the urge to retch every ten minutes would subside. Until then…Natalie let her eyes drift close, the heat only accentuating the fatigue that seemed to drag on her like a lead weight tied to her waist, and for a second she tuned out Nora's rant to rest. She was just slipping into a hazy dream state when a knock at the door interrupted them.

"If that's Dad, I'm leaving."

Natalie didn't have the energy to argue with her and merely nodded in understanding. The barbecue last week had been brutal. Natalie knew she owed Nora for agreeing to go, knowing full well their father would probably use the opportunity to lay in to his youngest daughter for something, anything. But at the moment she couldn't summon much more than resignation at the situation between them. She drew a deep breath and let her eyes close again.

Nora opened the door and, Natalie, half expecting it to be a neighbor, was almost positive her heart stopped beating when she realized who her sister was welcoming into her tiny apartment with a puzzled look on her face.

"Nat…did you lose a necklace?"

Fingers flying to her throat as if she'd just realized it was missing, her eyes bounced from the fine gold chain curled in Evan's palm to the boyishly handsome face she'd been doing her best to bury in the deepest, darkest corner of her memory, and she tried to breathe. He doesn't know. He couldn't. It was coincidence and an overdeveloped sense of Boy Scout values that brought him here, not the knowledge that she carried his child. But, even as she forced a smile despite the slight flutter of panic souring her empty stomach, the fact that he'd come personally to return something as small as a necklace was touching.

"Hello? Remember me? Apparently, I turned invisible." Nora turned to Evan, shaking her head, as she extended her hand. "I'm Natalie's younger sister, Nora. And you are…?"

"Just a friend," Natalie blurted, ignoring Evan's subtle frown. She turned to him with a bright smile. "Thanks so much for bringing this back to me, though you really shouldn't have gone to all the trouble. Can I get you some gas money or something?"

"Gas money?" Nora echoed incredulously. "Geez, Nat, he's not a taxi. Honestly, what's wrong with you? You're being rude." At that moment she didn't care. She was willing to sacrifice her manners to keep her sister from finding out Evan's identity but it was too late. Nora's curiosity had already been piqued. "Let's try this again—I'm Nora and you are…?"

"Evan Murphy. Pleased to meet you."

Natalie sent a fervent wish to God asking for the floor to swallow her whole, but apparently her request went straight to the Almighty's voice mail—there was no escaping the dawning light in her sister's eyes.

"Rafting-trip guy?"

"Unless she's met another by the same description," Evan answered and Natalie almost groaned out loud. He flashed a playful smile at her, as if sharing in a private joke, and it was all she could do not to glare at him for ruining her plan to ease him into the situation—according to her schedule.

"It is a *pleasure* to meet you." Nora extended her hand, a big smile on her face. "I've only recently learned of you. My sister is very closed-lipped about her friends. But

I can't understand why she'd want to keep you a secret. You seem…very nice."

"Nora," she warned, wishing a roll of duct tape were handy, "another time."

"Am I missing something?" Evan asked.

"Not at all. Just happy to finally meet you."

"Yes, now you've met him," Natalie said tightly before turning to Evan with a forced smile. "But, unfortunately, we were just leaving so I don't have time to visit. I'm sorry. Maybe if you'd called first—" *then I could've ensured this awkward visit never happened* "—we could've chatted longer."

The gentle rebuke was designed to make him reluctant to attempt another unannounced visit and it might've worked, except as he turned to leave Natalie caught a subtle whiff of his particular aftershave and she was overwhelmed by two nearly instantaneous reactions: the desire to bury her nose in his neck and the urge to vomit.

Her mouth watered and a pathetic moan followed, as she knew what was coming next. She must've paled, as both Nora and Evan came toward her though she waved them away.

"Nat? Are you all right?"

"I'm fine," she answered, the words coming out in controlled gasps as black spots danced before her eyes and the floor slanted under her feet. "I just…I just need…" Rest, she wanted to say—lots of it, and God, a glass of ice-cold water. Too bad she couldn't get her mouth to actually say the words. Instead, out came a mumbled mess and suddenly Evan was beside her moving more quickly than she'd have thought possible. Or perhaps she was moving in slow motion and it only seemed he was moving that fast…and then the black spots converged into one big ink blot and then there was nothing.

"Natalie!" Nora cried just as Natalie crumpled in Evan's arms, folding in a boneless heap across his forearm.

Drawing her to his chest, he carried Natalie to the sofa and gently deposited her while Nora ran to the telephone.

"Has she been sick?" he asked, gently pushing a chunk of sweat-dampened hair from her forehead. She didn't look very good. Her skin was clammy and her breathing shallow. When Nora didn't answer right away, his voice sharpened. "Nora?"

Nora looked suspiciously conflicted and

his concern grew. Memories of their short time together appeared with sharp clarity as he mentally flipped through their brief conversations, searching for a clue that perhaps she'd been ill.

Nora mumbled something that sounded like "sort of" and then he lost her attention as a dispatcher came on the line.

Sort of? How is a person "sort of" sick?

Staring down at the face that had dogged his steps since returning to California he couldn't help but feel as if he'd just fallen into the deep end of the pool without a life jacket. This wasn't how he pictured their reunion but he couldn't leave until he knew she was going to be all right.

THE SOUND OF SIRENS split the air and Natalie's eyelids fluttered. Footsteps pounded up the staircase and Nora opened the door so the paramedics could rush in. She struggled to sit up but Evan wouldn't let her. "Hold on, there…not until you get checked out."

"No—" she murmured with a decisive shake of her head, protesting as the paramedics began taking her blood pressure. "I don't need anyone checking anything."

"BP's a little on the high side," the paramedic said, looping the stethoscope over his neck to check her pupils with a penlight. "Are you taking any medication?"

"I'm fine, really…I'm just a little overheated. Nora, tell them I'm fine," she implored her sister.

"You're not fine," Evan disagreed, answering for Nora. "People don't faint for no apparent reason. If the paramedic says your blood pressure is high, maybe you ought to have it checked out."

"It's the heat," she insisted, trying to move away from the paramedics, flapping at them weakly when everyone moved to stop her. "I'm just a little overheated. Please don't make a big deal out of it. It's embarrassing."

"Ma'am, have you eaten at all today?" the paramedic asked, ignoring her request to be left alone. "Are you hypoglycemic or diabetic?"

Natalie shook her head, her face pallid despite the heat in the room.

The paramedic turned to Evan. "As far as I can tell, she's at the very least dehydrated. Her blood pressure is higher than normal and her heartbeat is erratic. But if she doesn't want to go we can't make her. Perhaps one of you can persuade her to go to the hospital."

Evan hesitated. He didn't really know this woman but worry overrode his good sense when he caught the wordless communication between the two sisters. He should walk away. Obviously, whatever was going on Natalie wanted to keep private but he felt an inexplicable need to stay.

"Nora, tell me what's going on."

Nora opened her mouth with an apology in her expression, and Natalie knew she was seconds away from revealing her secret if she didn't do something.

"If I agree to go to the hospital and get checked out will you stop worrying?"

In other words: *will you promise to keep your mouth shut?*

She expected the relieved smile from her sister but when Evan mirrored it she felt light-headed again. "But—" she struggled to sit up, resisting any assistance from Evan and sending a pointed look toward the paramedics who were waiting on her decision "—I'm not going in an ambulance."

"Fair enough," Evan said. "I'll drive you."

"Good idea," Nora chimed in before Natalie could protest. "I'll follow."

Despite the distinct feeling she'd just been sold out by her younger sister, Natalie had no choice but to go along. If she backed out now Evan would ask why and if she told him— her body shook making Evan tighten his hold to steady her—she'd lose her independence and, more than likely, any possibility of preserving the memory of their time together.

THE PLAN WAS to see her safely to a doctor and make his quiet departure, closing an awkward chapter to what he'd thought was going to be a pleasant reunion. But even as they'd wheeled her away for bloodwork, he'd chosen to wait with Nora. Leaving without saying goodbye felt too much like sneaking away so he opted to stay and found himself fielding an assortment of nosey questions.

"So, what do you do for a living?"

"I raft in the summer and teach skiing in the winter."

She frowned. "Is that all?"

"Excuse me?"

"I mean, it's just that it doesn't sound very

lucrative. Or maybe it is, I just can't imagine that it pays very well."

He bristled slightly. "I do well enough."

"Right." Her slow response gave him the distinct impression she was sizing him up—for what he couldn't imagine, but it made him uncomfortable. It wasn't the first time he'd been caught in the crosshairs of an eligible female and he knew the signs. A quick glance down at her bare fingers told him all he needed to know and he knew exactly how to shake her off his tail.

"I'm really more of a free spirit. A 9-to-5 job doesn't interest me," he said. "It's not my style. I like making my own hours, being my own boss."

She surprised him when she agreed. "Me, too." Then her brow furrowed. "But Natalie craves stability. I can only imagine that's the reason she stayed with Dan Gorlan for so long. Let me tell you, his leaving was a blessing in disguise. Honestly, I didn't think he had the stones to do something so bold but, boy, was I glad when he did." When Evan failed to comment, she returned to her previous train of thought. "I knew there had to be a good reason she didn't want to spill the beans. I practically had to drag it out of her," Nora said, completely missing the confounded look Evan sent her. She continued with a nod as if she'd just figured out some crucial component to the situation. "I'll bet right now she's probably too hung up on the fact you're a grown man doing a college kid's job. Is there any chance you could find a real job sometime soon?"

"I have a real job," he said, trying not to growl at the nosey woman. He was accustomed to John giving him hell for his choices, but he was stunned when a complete stranger started criticizing him.

"Let's be honest here. I wouldn't exactly say what you do is a serious occupation. River rafting is something kids do when they don't want to get a real job," Nora countered with a snort, and Evan's ears started to burn. She continued, matter-of-fact. "Natalie's former fiancé was an investment banker. Completely dull, if you ask me, but Natalie doesn't enjoy surprises. Hence, my astonishment at her involvement with someone like you."

Before he could tell her to mind her own business, the doctor returned, studying the folder in his hands.

"How is she?" Evan asked quickly, earning a speculative look from Nora.

"Doing better," the doctor replied, missing the quick exchange. "Her iron levels are low and she was certainly dehydrated. Has she been vomiting more than once an hour?"

"I think so," Nora answered. "When I came over she said she couldn't keep anything down. Is that normal?"

The doctor chuckled. "For a woman in her first trimester? Completely. It should pass in a few weeks but if it doesn't she might have a condition known as hyperemesis gravidarum. We're going to give her some IV fluids and that should perk her up a bit, and then when she's discharged make sure she gets some prenatal vitamins. It's never too early to start taking care of yourself when you're pregnant."

The doctor smiled and left, leaving Evan to stare after him. "Pregnant?"

"Yeah, that was my reaction, too," Nora said. Then added, "If Natalie asks, it wasn't me who talked, okay? But I'm so glad someone did because it was eating me alive." Seeing no further need for censure, she continued as if Evan wasn't staggering under the weight of the accidental disclosure. "When

Natalie told me I nearly swallowed my tongue. I mean, Natalie is the most responsible person on the planet. Well, she was until she came back from that rafting trip. I mean, she's probably the most Type-A person you'd ever meet under normal circumstances. Structure is very important to her. For crying out loud, she labels and dates her socks when she buys them so she knows which pairs go together." She paused, presumably to catch her breath, and continued without apology. "So, let's get down to brass tacks. We only have so much time before she gets back and she'll no doubt send me away when she finds out you know. I have to ask…did the condom break or what? I know, I know, it's none of my business and I don't want to know details but this whole Dan thing has thrown her for a loop. I mean…Natalie? River-rafting? If you knew her—"

"Whoa!" Evan interjected, his head spinning. "Hold on a minute, will you?" Had he slipped into the Twilight Zone? She looked annoyed at being interrupted but he didn't care. "Natalie's pregnant…and you think it's mine?"

"Try to keep up. And yes, I think you are the father of my sister's baby."

"That's impossible! We used protection," he blurted out, all sense of grace deserting him in one panic-stricken moment. Heat crawled into his cheeks. It wasn't his style to share the details of his sex life—no matter the circumstances. Recovering enough to try again, he continued, "Like I said…we were careful. I can't be the father."

"Condoms break."

"Well, mine didn't." Had it?

Nora shrugged. "Only abstinence is one hundred percent."

He didn't need a sex-ed talk. "I know that," he muttered. Why was he even discussing this with her? He'd have known if the condom had broken. "But it's not my baby."

"Are you calling my sister a liar?"

Evan met Nora's challenging stare. "I'm not calling anyone anything. But I'm very careful about those things."

"But like I said, if you knew Natalie—"

"We've already had this conversation," he interrupted, tension roughening his voice. "I don't mean to be insensitive but it isn't my baby. Maybe you don't know your sister as well as you think."

"Listen, buddy, you're lucky you even

know. Natalie was obviously dragging her feet about telling you, for whatever reason, but I didn't think it was right so don't make me regret breaking her confidence." Nora gave him a testy glare as if he were being unaccountably difficult. "As I was saying, if you knew Natalie you'd know she isn't the kind to sleep around. Honestly, I'm still a little shocked she slept with *you*."

"What's wrong with me?" he balked.

"Don't take it personally but you're really not her type."

He had the sense to not point out he was exactly her type two months ago but the temptation only made him more churlish. "What's your point?"

"My point is—"

Nora was interrupted by a nurse as she wheeled the gurney carrying Natalie into the room and helped her climb into the bed. They both approached her as the nurse left with a smile.

"How are you feeling, Nat?" Nora smoothed the hair from Natalie's forehead. "You really scared me. Don't do that again."

Residual anger stemming from his conversation with Nora kept him from talking just yet. Unfortunately, he didn't know who he was mad at the most—Nora for insulting him or Natalie for claiming she was pregnant with his child. Hailey's face burst out of his memories, and a scene as painful as it was ugly made him swallow reflexively. He'd spent years burying that particular memory and he had no interest in digging it back up again, but damned if he wasn't feeling the same sickness in his gut at the possibility he was catching a rerun. What if by some cruel cosmic joke it really was his baby?

Arms crossed, he watched the sisters talk, keenly aware Natalie was avoiding his stare. Guilty conscience? There was one way to find out.

"How are you feeling?"

Something was wrong. Evan's voice, though solicitous, was not warm, and her gaze flew to Nora's. Natalie searched her sister's face, praying that she'd kept her mouth shut. Nora lifted her shoulder in a helpless gesture and Natalie wanted to sink through the mattress. Nora! The woman couldn't keep a secret if her damn life depended on it. He knew. Now what?

"The doctor said you were dehydrated. Any particular reason?"

Natalie sighed. "Nora, can you give us a few minutes?"

"Are you sure you don't want me to stay?" Nora sent Evan a look that promised retribution if he so much as uttered the wrong word, but Natalie shook her head and she reluctantly left the room.

Once alone, Natalie met Evan's narrowed stare without flinching, though a part of her was sad to see the flint replace the kindness she'd seen earlier. "You know." He nodded, the gesture small but grave and packed with unspoken questions. She sighed. "I'm sorry."

"Sorry for what exactly?"

Natalie swallowed, his words cutting more than she'd thought they would. "I'm not sure," she answered honestly.

"What makes you think it's mine?" he asked, his voice hard. "I know for a fact we used protection."

Her eyes stung. She shouldn't have been hurt by his reaction but she was. She ground out the tears with her palm. "Don't you think I know that? Do you think I purposefully set out to get pregnant by a man I hardly know? By a man who makes his living ferrying tourists up and down a river? Give me a break!"

"So, there's no doubt?" he asked, the slight hope in his tone making her angry. He lifted his hands defensively. "Natalie, you know I have to ask. There's a lot at stake here.

"When were you going to tell me?" he asked, the planes of his face harsh.

Natalie swallowed. "When I was ready. I think," she added guiltily.

He made a sound of disgust and she lifted her chin despite knowing in her heart his anger was justified.

"Don't you think I had a right to know?"

Natalie made a short mirthless sound. What difference did it make now? He knew, and short of erasing his memory there was nothing she could do about it. Damn Nora for butting her nose into places it didn't belong.

"Natalie, answer me. Don't you think I had a right to know?"

A growing sense of self-preservation sharpened her voice as she met his cold gaze. "Yes, you had a right to know," she agreed. "But if you want me to be honest, I wasn't sure whether or not I was going to tell you and I wish you hadn't found out." His eyes widened at her blunt remark, but she waved him away. "So, now you know. Don't worry,

I don't want anything from you. You're off the hook, okay? Just go."

"Just go?" he repeated incredulously. "You expect me to walk out of this place knowing you're pregnant with my kid?"

"Yes." She looked away. "You can go on with your life and I won't bother you with the details of my pregnancy." Her pregnancy. Her baby. If it weren't for the sadness pulling at her, she might have enjoyed the subtle flutter she felt at the realization she was carrying another life inside her. Her palm strayed to her belly. Evan's gaze followed and she jerked her hand away.

His stare made her feel like a lab rat and she shifted uncomfortably. Hadn't she given him what most guys in his position would give their eyeteeth for? She didn't understand. Her frustration was evident in her tone as she continued, "If you're worried about child support, I do fine on my own. I don't need your money."

"Then what do you want?"

Natalie lifted her chin. "From you? Nothing."

CHAPTER ELEVEN

"FINE! HAVE IT your way. I'm outta here!"

The echo of his final words to Natalie reverberated in his mind no matter how hard he pushed himself. Evan rammed the post-hole digger deep into the ground, grunting with the effort it took to penetrate the baked topsoil. The action did little to stop the turmoil in his head or block the image of Natalie's stricken expression as he'd left her at the hospital, yet he continued to push himself harder in the hopes that it would.

Mending fences was grueling work but he welcomed the physical labor, hoping the strain on his muscles would blot out everything else. Except it didn't. Instead, he was alone in a field with nothing but the occasional hawk flying overhead and curious groundhog to break in to his thoughts. It was downright masochistic the way his mind wouldn't give him a moment's peace.

Natalie was carrying his child. It didn't make sense but somehow he knew she wasn't lying and the knowledge tapped a well of other questions. Was she taking care of herself? What if she had another one of those fainting spells when she was doing something like crossing the street or driving? He paused only long enough to drag the back of his hand across his forehead, then bent down to grab the pole lying beside him. As he lowered the thick piece of wood into the freshly dug hole, for a wild moment he considered calling Natalie to make sure she was eating properly and taking her vitamins, but stopped short when he remembered he was the last person she wanted to see or hear from again.

She said she didn't need him. He ought to just leave it at that. *So, drop it, already.* Irritated, he couldn't quite shake the unsettled feeling from his brain. He jerked the length of barbed wire taut and secured it before moving on. He told John he'd have the fence mended by night-fall, but if he didn't stop wasting valuable time arguing with himself over the situation with Natalie, he'd be eating his words—and he didn't have much of an appetite for crow.

Besides, Natalie had made it quite clear

how she felt about him. The sting that followed was unexpected. The solitude beckoned honesty and he had to admit the decision to go to Emmett's Mill had been grounded in something far more than courtesy. He'd wanted to see her again. And seconds before Nora opened the door, something in his gut had fluttered to life, reminding him of the excitement he'd experienced touching her skin and kissing her lips. Damn, if he hadn't craved just a taste of what they'd shared in Utah.

Instead, when he'd seen Natalie, sweat-dampened hair sticking to her face, looking like something the cat dragged in, what he'd thought was simple lust evaporated and genuine concern took its place.

He closed his eyes, briefly shutting out the blazing sun, his mind wandering.

Was it a girl? A boy? Would he or she favor his side of the family or Natalie's? How would she support a child? Did she have a nest egg? Nora said she was the orderly type...perhaps she was prepared for the unexpected. He didn't know her well enough to even speculate. Hell, after Hailey he didn't trust his ability to read anyone.

For all he knew, Natalie was nothing like she seemed.

He didn't learn Hailey was having an affair with his best friend, Randy, until the day he accidentally discovered the positive pregnancy test. His joy at becoming a father was soon eclipsed by a sickening sense of loss as she admitted the baby might not be his. Up until that point, he'd have sworn all was well. He couldn't have been more wrong. She packed her bags that day and aborted the eight-week-old fetus shortly after.

A spasm rippled through him as it always did when he happened to wander too close to the memory of his first brush with fatherhood. Aborted. Just like his dreams…his ambitions…his life.

A sickening thought followed. What if Natalie chose not to have the baby? He'd always believed it was a woman's right to choose, but having been on the other end, he knew what it felt like to stand by and watch helplessly as a life was snuffed out without consideration to the father's feelings. Hailey's justification had been that. Randy hadn't been interested in becoming a father and she wasn't about to jeopardize their budding relationship with the burden of an unwanted child.

Swallowing hard, he took a long moment to survey the finished work, his mind gratefully leaving behind the painful memories, and felt a small amount of satisfaction with the end result. If only fixing the broken spots in your life were as easy as mending a fence. He tossed his tools into the bed of his truck, knowing there wasn't enough wire in the world to shore up what was lying broken inside of him. There were just some things that couldn't be fixed…no matter how many times you tried.

NATALIE'S SHOULDERS ached from steaming the walls but she kept at it, needing to see more progress than she was getting in order to justify that she had made the right decision. The front door opened and she turned in the hope it was the deli delivery guy bringing the lunch she'd ordered a half hour ago.

Her smile disintegrated. "If you don't have a sandwich to deliver you can just walk right out the same way you came."

"It wasn't me who told him," Nora said,

storming toward her. "How many times do I have to tell you that?"

"We can talk about this later. I have work to do."

"When? When will we talk about it? You haven't returned my calls since that day in the hospital and you've no doubt been deleting my e-mails. How long are you going to stay mad at me for something I didn't do!"

"As long as I feel like it," she returned coolly, silently enjoying Nora's heartache. She knew it wasn't very sisterly but neither was selling one out—and as far as Natalie was concerned that was exactly what Nora did when she pushed the issue with Evan. Perhaps if she'd kept her mouth shut Evan would've left without finding out about the baby and Natalie could've preserved the memory of their time together. "And you might not have actually told him but you certainly didn't deny it when you had the chance to cover for me. I wasn't ready to tell him and now despite what I've told him he probably thinks I'm trying to trap him into some kind of relationship."

Nora snorted. "What relationship? I don't see him beating down your door. Seems to me like you got your wish after all. He's not around, so what's the big deal?"

"The big deal is, it wasn't your call. It was mine."

"You're right. I'm sorry. But if it counts for anything, my heart was in the right place. I just didn't want to see you lose out on something that might've been good."

Natalie's mouth twisted. "Like what? A shotgun wedding?"

"No," Nora answered softly. "A good guy."

An image of Evan's face, cold and remote, returned and Natalie bit down on her lip. "What makes you think he was a good guy? He left, remember?"

"You practically kicked him out of the hospital room," Nora pointed out with as much tact as her personality would allow. "It's not as if you extended much of an invitation to stick around."

Nora was right but Natalie wasn't ready to go there. "Well, if he cared he might've stayed no matter what I said to him."

"Nat, I've never known you to be such a…*girl*."

"You say it with such disdain. You're a girl, too, you know."

"Yeah, but when I say 'go' I don't mean 'stay.' I'm too old to play games like that and if I'm too old then you're *way* too old."

"We're only three years apart," Natalie retorted.

"Exactly."

Her mouth tightened and she returned to her steaming. Nora went to her side and talked over the hiss of the machinery doing its best to loosen the old wallpaper from the walls. "Nat…you need someone on your side. You can't do this alone."

"And why not?" she shot back stubbornly. "I'm completely capable. It's not as if I'm an invalid. What do I need anyone else for?"

"Well, for starters how about moral support?" Natalie shot her a derisive look and Nora quickly countered. "And a coach."

"A what?"

"A birthing coach."

Natalie's toes curled in the privacy of her shoes at the pain that followed as Nora's statement fully illuminated the fact she was completely alone. Good. *That's exactly how I want it,* a voice returned with only the slightest quiver.

"And," Nora said, no doubt knowing the

emotional leverage her next statement would have, "you're going to need someone to stand beside you when you tell Dad the news. You can't hide it forever."

"I know." She looked away, suddenly putting the steamer down. The hiss slowly gurgled to silence and it hung from her fingertips until she finally laid it on the floor. She never imagined the day she told her parents she was pregnant would feel anything like this. She wasn't sure if the queasy feeling in the pit of her stomach was a product of her overactive hormones or the disquiet that accompanied her thoughts when she considered approaching her family with the news.

"See?" Nora said. "You know how Dad's going to react. At least if I'm there, he won't know who to attack first."

"Why do you always make him out to be some kind of devil?" she asked, rubbing at a spot between her brows.

"Because most of the time—" Natalie gave a sharp shake of her head and Nora switched gears. "Listen, all I'm saying is, it won't hurt to have someone on your side."

"Are you on my side?" Natalie asked. "Because it sure didn't feel like it last week."

"I was trying to help."

"I don't need that kind of help. This is hard enough without having to run interference from you." She inhaled and blew out the breath slowly, digesting Nora's answer. Under normal circumstances, she probably wouldn't have stayed mad at her. Despite the hormones drenching her brain and moving her mind in terribly nauseating circles, she knew deep down Nora had truly been trying to do what she thought was right. But that was the problem with her younger sister—she never knew when to leave well enough alone. Unfortunately, as much as she wanted to nurse her anger a little bit longer, Nora had a point. Having someone with her to break the news to their parents was an idea with merit. "All right," she finally said, earning a relieved smile from Nora. "I forgive you. But if you pull anything remotely close to the stunt you pulled with Evan, I swear to God—"

"Don't worry, I've learned my lesson," she interrupted, though Natalie didn't believe it for a second. Nora pulled her sister into a fierce hug. "Thank you."

"You're welcome," Natalie answered

against Nora's shoulder, smiling in spite of her lingering irritation. She drew away. "Now, unless you're going to roll up your sleeves and help, get the hell out of here."

"I'll take a rain check, I promise," she said solemnly, raising her pinky finger. "If I didn't have a client meeting in fifteen minutes I'd gladly help."

"All right then, go play in someone's backyard." She tossed her head and Nora blew her a kiss before skipping out, only too happy to oblige.

Natalie sighed. She wasn't really angry at Nora but the feelings that had threatened to blossom at the first sight of Evan scared her. They had no future and it was best for everyone to understand that simple fact. She was having a stranger's baby. Aside from contributing to the little bump in her belly, they had nothing in common. Natalie suppressed a groan. *Way to go, Nat.* This was why she wasn't spontaneous. Obviously she was no good at it.

Her palm strayed to her still-flat belly and she fought against the awful loneliness sucking at her like stagnant swamp mud. What was Evan doing? Had he taken her offer to heart and begun the process of forgetting about her and the baby? She'd given him permission to walk away without strings. Obviously, he'd accepted. Her mouth tightened as an annoying wave of weepiness made her reach for the tissue box sitting on the nearest window ledge. *Stop it.* Nora was right. She had practically tossed him out on his ear, so why was she the one feeling rejected?

"So, WHAT'S THIS all about?" Her father's gruff voice penetrated Natalie's chaotic thoughts as she tried desperately to find a way to break the news gently. Yet she knew no matter how she phrased it, telling her father she was going to be an unwed mother had her palms sweating. His gaze swung to Nora, who was slowly swirling the remainder of her beer.

"Well? You two have been acting weird all night. Are you going to tell me what's going on or keep fiddle-farting around? Either get on with it or forget about it."

"Dad, what makes you think there's something going on?" Natalie forced a chuckle and tried to take a bite of her potato salad without choking. "Can't we come over for dinner just to enjoy your company?"

Gerald grunted as if he knew better, but didn't comment. Natalie shot a nervous look Nora's way. She couldn't do it. Her courage was slowly dripping out of her reserve and by the time her mother served the ice cream, there'd be nothing left for her to draw upon.

"Have you heard from Dan at all?" Missy asked, her expression mildly hopeful.

"Mom, Dan is history," Nora interjected, saving Natalie the effort. "Get used to it. Besides, Dan wasn't all that great anyway."

"Why do you say that?" Their mother's expression faltered as if Nora's comment had just rocked her foundation. "He seemed like a very nice, reliable young man."

Nora opened her mouth but Natalie jumped in, no more interested in discussing Dan's shortcomings than she was to blurt out that she was pregnant. But she was here for a purpose and if all hell was going to break loose, it might as well be for the right reasons. "Mom, Dad…I do have some news to share…." She looked to Nora for reassurance, then put on a brave face.

"I knew it," her father announced, his lips

set in a grim line. "Something's gone wrong with this new-fangled business venture. Well, spit it out."

Missy gasped. "Oh, Natalie! Is it true?"

From her peripheral vision Natalie caught Nora rolling her eyes and she knew she had about two seconds before the two started feuding. "Dad, please," she said, striving for a reasonable tone. "Nothing's wrong with the bookstore. In fact, I managed to get all the wallpaper down and the drywall guy is scheduled for next week. Everything's fine."

"Well, what is it then?"

Natalie hesitated and for a wild, brief moment she wished she hadn't chased Evan away, that he was right there beside her, ready to face the one-man firing squad her father could be when he was presented with something he disliked. True, she hadn't known him long, but Natalie suspected Evan could bear the brunt of her father's disapproval much easier than she. Her entire life had been spent earning her father's approval and she was about to lose it.

"Natalie?" Her mother ventured, her eyes darting between her two daughters. "What's your big announcement?"

A smile, formed out of desperation and an overall sense of impending panic, curved her lips. With false cheer and misplaced hope that she was truly overreacting, she announced, "I'm…uh, pregnant."

"Pregnant?" Missy gasped, her hands flying to her chest as if someone had just landed a roundhouse kick to her sternum. She regained her breath only to stammer, "But…but…you said Dan was…well, you're not together anymore."

"Uh, no, Dan and I are not a couple." Heat bloomed in her cheeks as she left the rest unsaid, hoping she didn't have to actually say out loud that she'd gotten pregnant by a one-night stand. Nora saved her by jumping in enthusiastically.

"Congratulations! You're going to be grandparents!" Nora exclaimed, the wide smile aimed at their father, who was staring at his plate as if the answers to life were hidden somewhere between his half-eaten pork chop and bread crust. "Oh, c'mon, don't be such a sourpuss for once. You're about to be a grandfather."

When Gerald refused to respond, Nora made a soft sound of disgust and stood to clear her spot. "We're not living in the Victorian age! So what's the big deal? She's having a baby…so what! People do it all the time, even lesbians have babies nowadays and no one seems to care there's not a husband or father around." Ignoring their mother's scandalized expression, she stalked to the kitchen with her dishes, leaving Natalie to wish she could follow.

She sent a nervous glance her father's way, noting the white lines bracketing his lips as he reluctantly met her imploring gaze. "Dad?" Natalie's voice cracked a little and she swallowed. "I know it's a surprise…." she said, but stopped as her father pushed away from the table, the abrupt motion causing a loud, protesting screech from the legs of his chair as they scraped against the linoleum. He walked away, the movement as stiff and unyielding as his personality. She looked to her mother, beseeching her help, but as always, Missy couldn't—or wouldn't—go against her husband.

Nora returned in time to see their father disappear into his office and slam the door, a stony expression twisting her fair features. She looked to Natalie, then their mother.

"Why does he have to be like that? Is it too much to be supportive? Loving? Mildly freaking interested in the things we do?"

Tears burned beneath Natalie's lids and her bottom lip trembled. Nora only saw the anger. Natalie sensed the bone-deep disappointment. Her father would never look at her the same.

And the knowledge almost sent her to her knees, begging for forgiveness.

But, as Nora and Tasha had already discovered, their father was not a forgiving man.

"I have to go," Natalie managed to choke out and headed toward the door in a jerky movement. "Nora?"

"Right behind you," her sister answered, hurrying to grab her purse.

"Natalie..." Missy began, but Natalie couldn't get out of there fast enough.

The door closed behind her and Natalie walked in tearful silence to Nora's Jetta, glad she'd agreed to Nora's offer to drive.

Nora climbed into the car, still ranting. "It's always the same song and dance with him. He never changes. We're not kids anymore. It's not his place to dictate how we're supposed to live our lives. He—" Nora looked over to see Natalie's shoulders shaking with silent tears. Her expression softened. "Nat? Are you okay?"

"Nothing will ever be the same," Natalie cried, wiping at the moisture on her cheeks in an angry motion. "Dad couldn't even look at me. Can you imagine how deeply I've disappointed him?"

"Who cares," Nora said with a shrug.

"I do," Natalie shot back. "I care!"

"Well, you shouldn't."

Natalie stared out the window. "What am I going to do without the support of my family?"

"Dad will come around," Nora said with a mild sigh tinged with annoyance. "And Mom will do whatever Dad thinks is best. So don't worry. It'll be fine."

She wished she shared Nora's optimism. But all she could see was her father's disappointment.

CHAPTER TWELVE

EVAN DIDN'T WANT to think about the ramifications of what he was about to do. All he knew was he couldn't walk away and he couldn't forget, which left him with one direction to travel: back to Emmett's Mill.

He'd spent the last two months punishing his body with hard, physical labor, doing all manner of odd jobs for John, in the hopes he'd eventually get to a place in his head that didn't feel as if he was selling his soul. But no matter how many times he fell into his bed, sore and exhausted, he couldn't move past the fact he had fathered a child.

The knowledge gnawed at his consciousness, dogged his every step and haunted his dreams. If that wasn't bad enough, memories of Hailey continued to resurface, reminding him of what could've been if he'd only fought harder and refused to give in.

He wasn't about to make the same mistake twice.

Hailey had robbed him of his child. He felt it in his bones. He couldn't do anything to change the past, but he could sure as hell make sure history didn't repeat itself. Pressing the gas pedal down just a hair harder, his truck picked up speed, roaring down the deserted road toward Emmett's Mill and the woman carrying his baby.

NATALIE OPENED her apartment door with a yawn, barely able to keep her eyelids open as she fumbled with the key lodged in the lock. She groaned as the key refused to disengage. She'd told Larry there were problems with the lock, but apparently, like her air-conditioning, the issue hadn't registered as serious enough to warrant attention. Running on a short fuse, she wiggled the key vigorously in an attempt to dislodge it, but to her horror the key snapped in her hand.

"Oh, nooo," she wailed, staring at the key, unable to believe the darn thing had broken off so easily. A test of the knob confirmed her fears. It was stuck in the locked position. If she closed her door, she'd never get it open again. Placing her purse between the door and the doorjamb so it didn't accidentally shut, she went downstairs to bang on Larry's door only to find a taped note.

Gone fishing. Be back next week. Slide rent under door.
L.

"Typical," she muttered, eyeing the offensive note as if it were to blame for her troubles and not the man who wrote it. She ought to complain. *Not that it would do any good.* Everyone knew Larry Tormendido was a lousy excuse for an apartment manager, but his family owned the small four-plex and as long as he didn't burn the place down, they left him to it. Natalie rubbed the back of her hand across her forehead, wiping away a sheen of sweat, as she contemplated her options.

The hardware store was closed, not that she knew how to get a broken key out of a door lock, but perhaps someone else might. She drew a deep breath as another wave of fatigue made her waver on her feet. Forget it, she thought, returning to her apartment. She'd just tape the deadlatch to the strike plate so that it couldn't actually engage and worry about it later. This was Emmett's Mill, not Fresno. She seriously doubted there was much to fear from burglars or rapists but if she didn't lie down for at least half an hour her eyes might permanently cross from exhaustion.

Making short work of taping the lock, she propped her purse against the door so it didn't swing open with the slight breeze, and collapsed on the sofa, her eyes closing before she even hit the cushions.

EVAN PULLED into Natalie's apartment complex, noting a sole vehicle in the diagonal slot marked for tenants, and glanced up at her open window. He didn't give himself the chance to stop and think, he just kept moving. Taking the steps two at a time, he came to her door and rapped his knuckles against the metal surface, startled when the door moved with the motion created by his hand.

He gave the door an exploratory push and it opened easily, a brown bag rolling and spilling its contents as if surrendering.

Sliding through the narrow gap, he stopped suddenly when he saw Natalie stretched out on the length of the sofa, gently snoring. Rooted to the carpet, he was unsure what to do. He glanced at the door and realized why it had swung open so easily. Why would she do that? Bending, he moved her purse out of the way and swung the door wider for a better look. Seconds later, he saw the broken key firmly lodged in the lock. He might've chuckled if he hadn't been wrestling with the urge to shake her for taking her safety for granted. Natalie shifted in her sleep, still oblivious to anything but her dreams, and Evan backed up quietly to let himself out. As he reached the lower level he glanced at the door to his left and saw the note taped there. He snorted with disgust. So much for calling on the manager to fix the problem.

He pursed his lips. There was only one solution. He'd have to fix it himself. *It's not your problem,* a voice argued. Yet, for the time being, it was. He couldn't leave knowing Natalie was sleeping in her apartment using a battered purse as her only defense against an intruder. His mama may have been dead, but he wouldn't put it past her to shake off the dirt and kick his ass if he left without trying to help. Even if Natalie didn't want his interference.

Too bad. She might as well get used to having him around because he wasn't going anywhere until they got this situation figured out.

NATALIE SLOWLY OPENED her eyes. She'd never known such lethargy in her life. Stiff from lying in an awkward position, she rose from the sofa and made her way to the kitchen for something cold to drink. As she passed by her answering machine, it indicated she'd received two calls. She pressed the button, listening with half an ear as she went through the motions of pouring herself a glass of water from the filtered canister she kept in the refrigerator.

Nora's voice broke the silence. With one breath she grumbled over their father's treatment at dinner the other night, and in the next she was suggesting they go to lunch. The call ended with a promise she'd call back later. *Terrific.* She lifted the glass to her lips and took a swallow. Nora meant well but Natalie's bruised feelings were still tender and she just wanted to be left alone. The next message was from a telemarketer, and she deleted it with an annoyed growl.

She was just putting her empty glass in the sink when the door opened and Evan walked in carrying a small plastic bag from the hardware store she'd thought was closed.

Skin itching from the sudden rush of adrenaline, she swallowed the shriek that popped in her throat.

"What are you doing? You scared me half to death. I could have you arrested," she added, still shaking. "This is called breaking and entering in case you didn't know."

"How long's this been broken?" he demanded, ignoring her threat. His mouth twisted in derision as he went on without benefit of an answer, bending one knee to start dismantling the doorknob. "Judging by the excellent care the manager takes in his rentals, no telling how long, I'd wager a guess. Am I wrong?"

A ridiculous urge to defend her absent apartment manager had her answering, though only God knew why. "It just broke this afternoon. Nothing like this has ever happened before. Evan, what are you doing here?"

"Fixing your doorknob. What's it look like?"

She frowned. She wasn't in the mood to play word games. Her exhaustion smothered the flutter of excitement that had flared to life the moment she'd seen him walk through the door, leaving cranky petulance in its wake. "I don't want you to fix my door. Stop it."

"And I don't want you to be pregnant with my kid. Sounds like we're both going to have to deal with disappointment. Shouldn't you be sitting down or something?"

"I'm not an invalid," she snapped.

"No, but the last time I was here—"

"That was different. I'd been throwing up all day and I was dehydrated."

"Has that changed?"

"A little," she admitted, then stopped. Why was she telling him anything about her bouts of morning sickness? In any case, for her a more appropriate title would be evening sickness. When six o'clock hit her mouth watered like Pavlov's dog with his stupid bell. As if to prove her point, saliva started filling her mouth and she had to swallow or risk drooling before she actually made it to the toilet. *Please, not now.*

"Are you okay?"

No, I'm about to embarrass myself by barfing on your Nikes. She was unprepared for the flicker of concern in his brown eyes. That minute glimmer was her undoing. She should've told him to mind his own business, but she didn't. "I'm fine," she answered reluctantly, adding with a small shrug, "It's hard to keep much down in the evenings."

"Do you need me to get you anything? Crackers? Club soda?"

For a brief instance, a yearning twisted through her as she imagined Evan's care was genuine and not rooted in the awkward circumstance between them. She remembered how sweet he'd been and a hesitant smile started to form on her lips, until another wave of nausea hit her, this time much stronger. She looked away, breaking the fragile moment between them.

"Evan, you never answered my question. What are you doing here?"

He returned to his task as if he was choosing to ignore her question, but his mouth had formed a tight line.

"Evan?" Exasperation colored her voice. "Don't ignore me."

He spared her a short look before sliding

the new knob into place and testing it with the key that came with it. "You can't go the entire weekend with a broken lock. If you're not going to take your safety seriously, I will. At least until we figure this out."

"And by 'this' you mean...?"

"The baby." He gave the knob a final twist before rising and tossing the key to her. She caught it with a startled motion and glared as she curled the metal in her palm. "And, you're welcome," he added when she failed to say anything.

"I didn't ask you to fix my door," she pointed out, knowing she sounded like a bratty child in the face of his actions. She bit back another defensive comment and instead grumbled her thanks. The thought of being able to properly close and lock her door was appealing. "But you didn't have to," she finished, needing some kind of last word on the issue.

"I get it," he said wryly as he took a seat on the sofa in a position that could almost qualify as lounging. Funny, Dan had never looked so completely at home in her cozy apartment. He'd been too busy complaining about the cramped quarters and her penchant for matching linens in the bathroom. "You're an independent woman and you don't need some man around to open pickle jars or lift heavy furniture."

Just one to fix broken door locks.

A ghost of a smile floated across his lips as if he'd just read her mind and she halted, disconcerted by the shiver that ran up her spine. Well, he had gorgeous eyes, she noted grudgingly. Honestly, he was more handsome than any man had a right to be. As far as the gene pool went, she'd certainly picked a winner. She instinctively drew back as she found herself wondering who their child would favor. Snapping back to reality with a jolt, she crossed her arms and gave him her best librarian stare, one that never failed to put unruly boys in their place no matter their age. She was practically sloshing with estrogen and it was messing with her brain.

"You should go."

"Not until we iron some things out."

"There's nothing to 'iron out' as you put it. I told you—"

"I can't walk away," he interrupted, meeting her stare, almost daring her to push him on the issue. She sensed his anger percolating under the surface, and she supposed she couldn't blame him. She certainly hadn't been on cloud nine when she'd realized she was pregnant but she'd offered—no, insisted—he take the easy-out clause. Yet, judging by the granite reflected in his expression, it would seem she'd done the exact opposite. Most men in his position would've been clicking their heels with relief, running through the open door so fast the action left little cartoon puffs of dust in its wake, but Evan seemed…offended.

"You have to," she answered abruptly, reacting to the confusion Evan had created in her mind. Did he want to be a father? "It's my decision."

"Not when half of that kid's DNA is mine," he maintained stubbornly, making her want to stomp her foot or grind her teeth in some adolescent display of frustration.

"Evan, it's not that simple," she said.

"It is to me."

They stood, facing off, and for a long moment she suffered an ache that followed his declaration. He wasn't supposed to come back. He wasn't supposed to care so much.

"Why are you doing this?" she whispered,

her voice cracking. "I don't understand. A baby will change your life forever. I'm offering you the chance to walk away before you have to get involved."

"It's not your right to decide my level of involvement with my child," he said quietly, his answer sending an arrow of shame shafting through her heart.

Evan was right but she had to do what was best for their child. She suspected Evan's heart was in the right place but it took more than just good intentions to raise a child. A child needed stability and a solid foundation. How could Evan possibly provide that when he zipped off for months at a time to play on the slopes or float down a river in another state? Her heart whispered that she was over-thinking the situation, that for once she should listen to what she felt inside but as she considered the possibility, the unknown loomed before her, reinforcing her belief that she needed to do what was practical…even if it wasn't the most romantic decision available. She didn't have the luxury of considering what Evan wanted in this situation.

She drew a deep breath. "Evan, I'm considering giving up the baby for adoption," she lied, looking away so he didn't read the truth in her eyes. "I think that might be best for everyone."

IN THE MOMENTS that followed Natalie's bombshell, two scenarios flashed through Evan's head with almost supernatural speed. In one, he ran to an attorney to draft paperwork preventing her from following through with an adoption; and in the second, he simply pulled her to a courthouse for a quickie marriage.

Okay, so the second one wasn't really a valid solution but was one created out of panic as he envisioned his child being raised under someone else's hand, in someone else's home. For a wild, infinitesimal second it gave him pause.

"Evan? Did you hear me?" Her voice cut through the circuitry of his brain, prompting a slow contemplative answer as he returned to reality.

"No."

"No?"

He met her incredulous stare.

She stiffened and crossed her arms. "What do you mean 'no'?"

"I mean *no*. You can't put the baby up for adoption without my permission and I can tell you right now, that isn't going to happen so forget about it. Case closed."

"You don't have any say in my decision," she countered indignantly, two hot points of color rushing to her cheeks. If he hadn't been pretty damn angry himself, he might've enjoyed the show.

"I have every right. That's my baby and if necessary we'll get a paternity test just to prove it for legal purposes. And there's no way in hell I'm going to let some stranger walk off with my kid. It's bad enough I have to share with you."

Natalie opened her mouth, outrage and something that looked like hurt reflecting in her eyes, but Evan couldn't let that get to him. This was the woman who was trying to pawn off his baby to a complete stranger; not the vulnerable traveler who'd captivated him with the shy looks she'd sent his way or the absolutely no-regrets sex they'd shared under cover of the Utah sky. He gritted his teeth as an erection stirred to life with the helpful imagery stuck in his memory and channeled his inappropriate desire into something more useful, like anger.

"When's the earliest you can have a paternity test?"

"I already told you it's your baby," she spat out, looking away as if the very sight of him made her stomach roll.

"And I believe you but I think since we're not married and not likely to get married before the baby's born, it's probably best to get a paternity test done for the paperwork."

"You want one so badly, you find out. Unlike you, I have a full-time job trying to open a bookstore on time."

"The same one you talked about in Utah? The children's bookstore?" he asked, distracted by his own interest. When she gave him a stiff nod, he almost gave in to the urge to congratulate her for taking a chance on herself, until her stony expression reminded him where they were. "Let's get down to the nitty gritty. What are your finances like?"

"None of your business," Natalie answered. When he gave her a look she relented reluctantly. "I'm fine. I took out a SBA loan and I padded it so I could live off it for a little while in case the bookstore didn't take off right away."

"Smart," he murmured, glad to see she had

a head for practicalities. He shifted, adding, "You won't be alone, Natalie…if that's what you're worried about."

Evan caught the subtle expression of sadness before she looked away and knew she wanted more for her child than a support payment. He dropped his gaze to the floor, weighing his words carefully, sensing a thoughtless word could ruin the incredibly small window that had cracked open. "I make decent money, more than enough to help support a child, and my job is such that I can take off long stretches of time. I'll be there."

Natalie's shoulders dropped a little as she let out a long pent-up sigh, her brows furrowing. "It's not that easy, Evan. We're talking about a child, not a puppy. A child who deserves a loving home with two parents. That's something you and I can't give this baby."

"Why not?" he asked.

She made an exasperated noise. "Evan, think about it. We didn't even know each other before Utah. And the time we did share was abbreviated…certainly not enough to determine whether either one of us is ready to be a parent. What we shared…was a short-term thing. Something neither one of us thought was going to turn in to anything else." When he didn't say anything, she continued with a drawn breath. "Trust me, I think this is for the best. For everyone."

I think this is for the best…the echo of Hailey's voice sliced through his thoughts and put an immediate chill on anything that resembled consideration to Natalie's logic. The blood started to pound in his ears as his heart rate increased. Nobody ever gave a damn what was best for him. Hailey surely hadn't. Natalie's voice moved over him in a jumbled mash of words, but he'd stopped listening.

He didn't care about what was best, he wanted to shout, but he didn't. He kept the words locked behind his teeth, the only evidence of his internal combustion was the tight press of his lips and the tic in his jaw. It might be an easy thing for her to give away her child but the very thought made him ill. He rose slowly, meeting her gaze as she searched his, the wild hope in her eyes making him feel bitter and twisted inside. He hated that whatever memory he had of her was now tainted with the realization that she was as cold as Hailey.

"I want a paternity test as soon as possible.

Until then, nothing changes. And if I find out you've moved on the adoption idea I'll slap you with a lawsuit so fast your head will spin. Trust me on this," he finished in a low growl. Without waiting for her response, he let himself out, needing distance, feeling sick and all manner of terrible things as he stalked to the truck and gunned the engine, anxious to escape the feeling in his gut and the weight in his heart. Right, wrong or indifferent, no one was going to take his kid from him.

CHAPTER THIRTEEN

"AND THEN HE just left!" Natalie finished indignantly as Nora continued to fiddle with the new lock Evan had installed. "Are you listening to me? The look in his eyes was downright scary. I mean, what kind of guy is that?"

"A guy who's pretty handy with a screwdriver," she answered, continuing to survey the lock. Natalie frowned and Nora gestured to the mechanism. "No, really, there's not a scratch on the plate or anything. And, it's a way better lock than that chintzy one you had before. I don't know, Nat…you might think about keeping him around instead of running him off all the time."

"You haven't listened to a word I've been saying," Natalie said, falling into her recliner with a glower. "I don't even know why I waste my breath sometimes."

Nora straightened and closed the door, passing by Natalie with an amused chuckle. "Man, those hormones have you channeling someone who's lost her sense of humor."

"What's to laugh about? I have a man practically stalking me because I'm carrying his child, my father has lost all faith in me and refuses to even look at me, and I have a sister who thinks all of this is *hilarious*. My life is just peachy. What's not to be just a teensy bit grouchy over?"

Nora grabbed two glasses and filled them with ice before adding purified water from the canister. She handed Natalie a glass, which she accepted with a grumbled thanks. Nora took a deep, satisfying swig, then eyed the broken swamp cooler unit. "Think he could fix this piece of crap?"

Natalie groaned. "Shut up. He's enough trouble as it is. I don't need to start tapping him for a handyman. Besides, with the weather changing I don't even need it anymore."

Nora shrugged as if conceding the point and took a seat opposite Natalie, who was lolling in her chair, feeling about as limp as a dehydrated houseplant.

"So, let me get this straight, you're mad

because he was mad for not liking your idea of giving away his baby. Is that about the long and short of it?"

"No-o-o," Natalie returned with annoyance. "I'm mad because he's being selfish and unreasonable."

"Because it's not the least bit selfish for you to keep his child from him even when he's expressed a strong desire to be a father to this kid?"

"He's not father material," she shot back, hating the logic of Nora's blunt observation.

"Neither is ours but it didn't keep him from fathering three."

"Stop it," Natalie said, a level of warning in her tone. "This isn't about our dad, it's about—" her gaze dropped to her belly and she was perplexed by what to call her tiny bump "—someone else's," she finished lamely.

"Yeah, well, all I'm saying is he can't be half as bad as ours."

Natalie bit down on her tongue, knowing Nora would gleefully jump into a discussion about the shortcomings of their father, and frankly, she didn't want to hear it. Their father was gruff, certainly, but apparently, Nora didn't remember the times that were mixed with kindness and there was no amount of convincing otherwise. She raised the cool glass to her forehead and enjoyed the minute comfort it offered. Lately, she felt like an oven, no matter that the cool October temperatures were brisk enough to encourage grabbing a jacket before going outside. "I'll have Larry look at the cooler as soon as he returns from his fishing trip," she said. Nora snorted as if she knew just how effective the manager really was and drained her glass. "I'll stake out his apartment if I have to," she grumbled.

"You do that." Nora rose to put her glass away and refill Natalie's. "In the meantime, I think you'd better give Evan's feelings some thought. He sounds as if he won't go down without a fight and that could get ugly. That's not what you want, is it?"

"It's my baby," she said stubbornly.

Nora shook her head, moving to the door. "Not just yours. And something tells me, that's not something he's bound to forget anytime soon."

There was nothing Natalie could say to refute Nora's statement, because it was true.

"I'll stop by tomorrow to check up on you, okay?"

"Sure." She offered a wan smile, the action simply for Nora's benefit, as her sister let herself out. The door closed behind her and Natalie let her head drop back on the headrest. What a fine mess…

WEEKS LATER, after a day at the store, Natalie chewed her bottom lip as she used the library computer to peruse the Internet for information on prenatal DNA testing before heading home. There was an independent lab that could perform the test as early as fourteen weeks through amniocentesis. According to the nurse practitioner at the maternity clinic, she was already twenty weeks. She frowned in distress. She wasn't wild about a giant needle poking through her belly button to her baby. But Evan was pretty adamant about the test even though she knew he didn't doubt her word. The fact that he wanted it simply for legal purposes should've made her feel better, but it didn't. It just hit home the fact that they were virtual strangers about to have a baby. She glanced at the clock and acknowledged Marilyn's signal that it was about time to lock up.

She sighed and her mind stubbornly

returned to the one subject she'd been duti-
fully ignoring. It'd been exactly fifteen days
since Evan had stormed out of her apartment
and each time she closed her eyes she saw his
expression, twisted and bleak, staring back at
her. It was a far cry from the soft visual
caresses she'd received in Utah. She'd give
anything to bask in that uncomplicated
warmth just once more. The memory of her
river-rafting trip seemed distant, almost
surreal. Something that hadn't actually
happened except in the privacy of her mind.
But the burgeoning bump on her belly was
proof enough that she had enjoyed a wild
ride in more ways than one. Her cheeks
burned at the imagery that popped with little
invitation and caused her to glance around
guiltily, as if someone might actually have
access to the carnal pictures locked in her
head.

The ride home was the most enjoyable part
of her day. She drove with the windows
down, even though November in Emmett's
Mill was hardly what anyone would call
warm. Storm clouds frequently gathered on
the horizon, threatening rain at any second,
but most times she was incredibly warm and

she loved the brisk feel of the wind in her face. She sang along to the song on the radio and bounced in her seat to the rhythm, completely oblivious to everything but the ride and the music.

She pulled in to her diagonal space and, waiting until she finished the last verse with a little gusto, she smiled broadly at her own off-key note and grabbed her purse before exiting. There was a truck parked in the slot two spots over, loaded with a few items, but Natalie gave it only a cursory glance, figuring Larry had finally found a tenant for the apartment directly below her. She didn't care as long as they were quiet.

Her good mood quickly evaporated with the onslaught of heat and she was anxious to remove her work clothes, which consisted of long, baggy overalls splattered with all manner of remodeling garbage and a short-sleeved shirt that had recently become too tight across her breasts.

She started up the steps only to slow suddenly—something about the truck seeming familiar. She stopped and tilted her head, wondering what had triggered the sense, then when nothing came immediately to mind, she shrugged and finished the short trek to her apartment.

Closing the door, she flipped on every fan she had and headed for the bedroom, stripping as she went.

Standing before her full-length mirror, she stared hard at her body, marveling at the changes. Her stomach was rounding noticeably and her waist was thickening. Tracing her fingers down her belly, she couldn't help but wonder how Evan would be with a woman he chose to have a child with. Sudden tears pricked her eyes when a sense of loss followed. What was wrong with her? One minute she felt on top of the world, the next she was ready to bawl her eyes out. This hormone business was no laughing matter. Inhaling with a watery hiccup, she grabbed a baggy T-shirt and some loose shorts and padded into the kitchen for something to drink.

Just as she bent her head to the fridge to survey her options, a loud bang outside drew her attention. Crossing to the window, she looked down and gasped. If she'd been holding anything in her hand she surely would've dropped it for directly below her, cursing like a sailor as he muscled a large bed frame from the back of his truck, was Evan.

HE COULD'VE JUST rented a motel room for a few months, which would've removed the need for furniture, but when he'd found out that the apartment directly below Natalie's was vacant, he didn't even think twice. Calling up the property management firm, it was easy work to procure the small apartment. He gave a short no-frills explanation to John about the situation he was in when his brother had discovered him loading up the truck, and for once John hadn't grilled him for details. He'd have to thank him for that later.

The knowledge that Natalie was considering adoption spooked him and he wasn't going to be more than a stone's throw away from her while she was pregnant. Rubbing the sweat from his eyes, he glanced up at Natalie's open window and saw her standing there, staring with a slack jaw. An unwelcome flutter jostled his insides and he turned away to heft the headrest.

Two seconds after he'd set the headrest down and mopped the moisture from his forehead, Natalie appeared at his doorstep, her expression stuck somewhere between alarmed and bewildered. "What are you doing?"

"Seems that's a popular question these days," he answered, drawing a deep breath before meeting her gaze. He squinted against the sunlight pouring in from the front window and made a mental note to purchase some cheap blinds. She recovered from the initial shock of seeing him again and crossed her arms against her chest, which only drew his attention more. It didn't take X-ray vision to see she was braless and, thanks to his fertile imagination and steel-trap memory, he was having a hard time concentrating. He cleared his throat and continued gruffly. "Just doing what I felt was necessary."

"Which is…?"

"Moving in."

"Are you nuts?" she gasped, her eyes widening in her shock. "You can't just move in."

"My deposit begs to differ," he said, grabbing a box and transferring it out of the way before walking past her to grab more stuff from his truck. "Watch yourself."

She took a faltering step backward but he could feel her steady stare on his back. He tried to ignore it but the effort was useless. He could almost see the energy vibrating inside her and he remembered quite vividly just how explosive it felt to be pressed up against her.

"Here's how I see it," he began, returning with another box and putting it in the corner before he headed back to the truck with the efficiency of one accustomed to hard work. "There's no way I'm going to be an hour or so away while you're pregnant. What if you collapse or need to get to the hospital and there's no one there to take you?" When she made a noise of protest, he shook his head. "Shit happens but it's not going to happen on my watch. That's a promise."

He looked over just in time to watch the rigid line of her jaw soften and he had to jerk his gaze elsewhere. He wasn't here for anything but the baby. He'd figure everything else out later. "So, for the time being…we're going to be neighbors."

Her mouth opened as if preparing to say something but Evan was too distracted by the soft pink flesh to actually hear if words had come out. He shook his head free of the inappropriate lust clouding his brain and focused on what she was trying to say, but as far as he could tell, she wasn't really saying anything coherent.

"Are you all right?" he asked, concern overriding everything else.

"I have to go," she stammered before turning on her heel and disappearing up the short flight of stairs, leaving Evan to stare after her, wondering if he should follow. The door slammed and he smiled. Well, that answered that question. It was just as well, he realized. He wanted to get everything moved in and set up by nightfall and that only gave him a few more hours.

Tonight, he'd be sleeping beneath Natalie—but it sure as hell wasn't as memory served or his imagination offered.

He groaned in annoyance, shifted the growing erection in his pants and brutally pushed all thoughts of Natalie from his mind. He might've just made things a whole helluva lot worse but what was done was done and there was no backing down now, even if he wanted to, which, he realized with a start, he really didn't.

CHAPTER FOURTEEN

NATALIE HAD ONLY just settled into a comfortable spot on the sofa when a soft knock at the front door startled her. Caught between a contradictory hope and concern that it was Evan, she climbed from the sofa and raked her hand through her hair before opening the door.

"Mom?" she said, surprised to see Missy standing there in her breezeway.

"Hello, Natalie, am I coming at a bad time?" she asked, giving her a warm smile even as she assessed her critically. "How are you feeling?"

"Um, fine, come on in," she said, gesturing. "What are you doing here?"

"I was in the neighborhood," Missy answered with a shrug, moving past her and into the living room to take a seat. "Now, tell me how you've been. You haven't been by since…"

"Since I dropped the news I was pregnant," she finished for her. Missy had the grace to look contrite though it gave Natalie no sense of satisfaction. She wanted the gesture to come from her father. "Well, I didn't feel welcome anymore."

"Don't be silly," Missy admonished. "You're always welcome in our home. You should know that. We were just surprised by your news, is all." When Natalie didn't respond, Missy assumed they were moving forward and smiled. "Tell me how you're feeling."

Natalie lifted her shoulders in a shrug. "Pregnancy isn't for wimps, that's for sure. Where's Dad?"

"He's at the retired chiefs meeting. You know, he wouldn't miss those for the world. He hates not being part of the action."

Natalie murmured her understanding but an awkward silence followed. They'd never been close and she found it weird that her mother was making this effort.

"Have you seen a doctor yet?"

"Yes, well, sort of," she quickly amended as a troubled frown pulled at Missy's brows. "I've seen the nurse practitioner at the OB/GYN clinic but I haven't actually seen a doctor yet. I guess that's pretty common. There are so many patients it's just easier and more efficient to do it this way. According to their little slide chart, my due date is March eighth."

Missy sighed, a wealth of resignation in the sound. "Well, it'll be here before you know it." A forced chuckle followed. "I can't believe I'm going to be a grandmother."

"Does that bother you?" Natalie asked.

"Oh, of course not," Missy answered quickly, though she continued as if she were trying to convince herself. "Many of my friends already have grandchildren. It's a natural progression. Although…I don't feel old enough yet to be a grandmother," she added, patting her hair absently before giving Natalie a smile that looked a tad strained.

"Mom, I didn't get pregnant on purpose," she found herself saying defensively, until Missy shook her head in understanding.

"Most pregnancies are unplanned, sweetheart. It happens. And, most of the time, it's wonderful."

"Really?"

Missy faltered for a second as if questioning her own counsel, then her lips curved in a bright smile. "Of course. I have three beautiful girls and I don't regret any of them."

"You're saying we were unplanned?" Natalie asked in shock, watching her mother curiously.

Missy lifted her shoulder in way of an admission and Natalie exclaimed as if scandalized by the information.

"What?" she asked innocently. "We were young once, too."

They shared a laugh and the mood lightened. Missy glanced at her watch and noted the hour. "I should get going," she said, rising.

"Gotta get back before Dad realizes where you are?" Natalie asked, unable to disguise the hurt in her tone. "What would he say if he knew you were here?"

Missy sighed. "He's been through a lot, Natalie. Give him time. He'll come around."

"Like he did for Tasha?" Natalie bit her lip, revealing her fear, but there was little Missy could say on that score. Gerald hadn't spoken to his eldest daughter in over ten years. The rift had torn apart their family in ways that would always carry a scar.

"This is completely different," Missy countered with conviction, but she continued in a strident tone, "Besides, it's Tasha's choice as well to stay away. Your father is not such a terrible ogre that he would deny Tasha back in to this family. Part of her absence is her decision. Remember that."

Natalie stared at her mother. "You know it's not that simple."

"It is if you make it so."

"Mom…" she began, ready to defend Tasha if only to remind her mother why she'd felt compelled to leave—no, run from—Emmett's Mill, but Missy wasn't interested and had begun walking toward the door.

"Drink lots of fluids," Missy advised, her hand on the doorknob. "And take your prenatals. Pregnancy takes a toll on the mother but it's worth it when you're holding that baby in your arms."

Natalie nodded at the advice and watched as her mother descended the stairs, then stopped as if remembering something. She turned. "Oh, I expect to see you and Nora at Thanksgiving. Aunt Jane is coming. Please tell your sister. I'm not sure if I'll see her in time."

"TELL ME AGAIN why we're here?" Nora asked, standing beside Natalie just as she knocked on their parents' door.

"Because," she answered, adjusting the cherry pie in her other hand for a better grip, "the offer was extended and I thought it might be a good way to end the discord." Nora gave her a blank stare and she added, "Oh, c'mon, at least it's free food!"

"Yeah, well I'm past the stage where free food moves me. I'm only here for that moral support I touted to get back in your good graces. This ought to count for at least ten brownie points."

Natalie sighed. "Duly noted. Now shut up and act happy."

The door opened and to Nora's credit, she pasted a smile on her face as their mother ushered them into the warm house that smelled of holidays past and instantly made her glad she'd decided to come. Even if her father wasn't full of sunshine, she'd enjoy the olive branch her mother had extended in the spirit of hope. It was the least she could do for her mother's intervention, which, even if Nora didn't recognize it as such, was their mother's gift to them all.

CHAPTER FIFTEEN

THANKSGIVING at the Murphy house was a crowded affair due to the intervention of Gladys Stemming.

Evan accepted a cup of something hot with a cinnamon stick sticking out the top and took a measured sip. "What is this?" he asked John, grimacing at the odd taste while surveying the assortment of neighbors milling about the house.

"Mulled cider...I think," John answered, taking out his cinnamon stick with a quizzical look. "Are we supposed to eat this or what?"

"You got me. Just stick it back in your mug before someone notices." Too late. Gladys was hot-footing it their way, a giant smile on her plump face. "Gladys, two o'clock," he managed to mumble out the side of his mouth to John before Gladys wrapped him in an expansive hug that nearly squeezed the air out of his lungs. "Gladys, you look fantastic," he said once she turned him loose and he could breathe again.

"You don't look half-bad yourself. You, either, Johnny boy," she said before settling between them to link arms. "Now, tell me what you think of the party. Be honest now."

"It's great," Evan answered before John could open his mouth. "How'd you talk all these people into coming? I don't think I've seen half of them in years."

"Oh, sweetie, I've been trying to get your brother to host a party at the ranch for a while now. Everyone loves what you boys have done here and I'll just bet your momma is pleased as punch that you've decided to finally rejoin the community."

Evan sent John a look as if to ask what the heck she was talking about, but John took the opportunity to sip more cider rather than answer.

"And guess who else is here?" She looked pointedly at John but didn't wait for a reply, continuing with a sweet, yet suggestive, smile. "Anna Morgan. I promised her a cup of cider but haven't had the chance to get it to her yet. Would you be a dear and get her some?"

Evan withheld a guffaw as his brother colored a few shades of magenta, but otherwise agreed and quickly disappeared. Gladys wore a pleased expression that could only mean one thing. The woman was trying her hand at matchmaking.

"What are you up to?" he asked, amused.

"Nothing that didn't need to be done in the first place," she said resolutely, watching as John made his way toward the redhead admiring the riding arena from the wide living room window. "That boy wouldn't know how to make the first move if it came to him with written instructions. He's been eyeing Anna since she moved here but he's too darn set in his own ways to consider trying anything. I'm just helping things along." She turned to Evan, eyes alight with interest. "What about you? I heard you were sweet on that cutie we met on the river. Natalie…that was her name. Great girl…a little on the rigid side but she seemed to loosen up by the end. In fact, she seemed a little sweet on you, too. Anything spark to life between the two of you?"

"You could say that," he admitted slowly, wondering if he should spill the beans.

When she poked him in the gut for obviously withholding information, he grunted. "Uh, well, she…"

"Spit it out, boy. I'm not getting any younger and if I know Hilda Bradshaw she'll start hitting the rum soon and we all want to avoid that display."

"She's pregnant," he blurted, still rubbing his midsection. "And, well, uh, it's mine."

"Evan Jeremiah Murphy," she gasped, her hand flying to her chest. "When I told you to be nice to the girl I didn't expect you to take it so far! Pregnant? Oh, lordy." She inhaled deeply and stared him down. "Well, are you going to marry the girl? Make an honest woman out of her?"

"Gladys…it's not that simple. We're not exactly a couple."

Her mouth turned down but she seemed to accept his answer…for a split second. Turning, she said, "I'm only going to say this once because you're a big boy and you don't need some old lady telling you what to do but I'm going to say what I think your momma would say if she were here."

Evan winced, pretty sure what his mom would say to him in this instance, but out of respect kept his mouth shut and waited apprehensively for the verbal butt-kicking that was surely coming his way.

"Your momma would've dearly loved being a grandmother," Gladys began, her voice lowering so only she and Evan were privy to what she had to say. "And I know she would've wanted you to do what's right for this baby. A child deserves two parents, but it's important for those parents to love each other as much as they love that child. If you think you can love Natalie, you owe it to the both of you to give it a try. Chances are, she's confused and scared and without knowing how you feel about her probably just makes things worse."

"I know," he answered with sincerity, wishing he could make the situation with Natalie easier to figure out. "But, I don't know how I feel." He gave a mirthless chuckle, admitting, "Natalie's not the only one scared and confused."

Gladys's face crinkled in a warm smile as she cupped his jaw with love in her eyes. "Evan…you have a good and pure heart. Try listening to it—it won't steer you wrong. I promise."

"I was wrong about Hailey," he reminded her darkly.

"That wasn't love," she said, shaking her head. "That was a...learning experience."

Wicked learning curve, he thought wryly, but gave her a smile to say he accepted her advice in the spirit it was given. Gladys gave his jaw a light slap and then shook his chin as if he were five, saying, "Lighten up, sweetie. It's a party! You'll figure things out. You always do."

Gladys took her leave, ostensibly to prevent Hilda from locating the rum hidden in the pantry, and Evan sighed heavily. If only he shared her confidence. These days he wasn't sure about much and that was a terrible feeling.

EVAN PULLED the bag of groceries from the bench seat in his truck and strode to his new apartment, the advice Gladys had given still echoing in his head even as he took note of the sad state of the building. It was hardly the best place to raise a child. For that matter, he wouldn't bring a puppy into this dump. Neither the landlord nor the manager seemed to care much about the building's upkeep but, even so, it served his purposes well.

Since taking residence, he'd managed to find a few pieces of furniture at the second-hand store, and his place was comfortable, if not fashionable. He'd even found a few pots and pans that didn't look like the ones Jonesy used to throw together their meals on the river.

Unloading the fresh vegetables and skinless chicken breasts he'd bought for dinner, he wondered what Natalie was eating tonight. As much as he tried to ignore it, Gladys's voice rang in his ears about giving things a shot. He was still attracted to her, at least they didn't have that problem. Or, he thought, maybe that was an entirely *different* problem, depending on how you looked at it.

His gaze traveled to the ceiling, listening with half an ear for movement. When he didn't hear any, he continued with his task. Once everything was on the counter, he sent another glance toward the ceiling. He knew she was home—her car was parked where it always was each evening—but there was little sound coming from the upper level, which was odd since the thin walls usually painted an audio picture with every little noise the residents made. He rested his hands on his hips as he contemplated banging on her door. What if she'd had one of those fainting spells again? A vision of Natalie lying unconscious on her carpeted floor had him moving to the door and up the stairs before he even realized what he was doing. Knocking softly, in case she was just sleeping, he was surprised when a soft voice answered from behind the door.

"Who is it?"

"Evan. Are you all right?"

A long pause, then a mournful sigh. "I'm fine. Go back downstairs, Evan."

He ignored her direction and opened the door, frowning when he noted it was unlocked. "I fixed this for a reason," he started to say until he saw Natalie curled up on the sofa, a box of tissues beside her and a pillow, sodden and splotched with her tears, hugged to her chest. She sniffed and tried burying her face. "Don't you ever listen? I told you to go away," she said, her voice muffled.

"What's wrong?" He came to her side and gently pulled the pillow from her face. "Is there something wrong with the baby?" he asked, a frisson of alarm coloring his voice.

Natalie made an exasperated noise and

pulled the pillow out of his grasp. "The baby's fine. It's me that's all messed up."

"How so?" he asked, earning a dark look before she blew her nose into the tissue. He handed her the box. "What happened to that independent woman I left behind a few days ago?"

Natalie stared at her knuckles as they curled around the fresh tissue and bit her lip, making him want to kiss it despite the fact that she hardly looked appealing with her matching set of puffy eyes and nose swollen from crying. She looked so wretched, he couldn't help but gently push a lock of hair behind her ear and out of her line of sight. She looked up quickly, surprised by the action, causing him to chuckle wryly. "You and me both. Now tell me what's going on."

She stared as if not quite sure she wanted to share and Evan didn't exactly blame her. Their relationship, if you could call it that, was nothing if not turbulent. They were going about the whole thing backward. He should've regretted the sex, seeing as where it had put them, but strangely, he didn't. When he thought of their time in Utah, a feeling of peaceful warmth pervaded his body—sort of the way he felt right now. He risked a glance at Natalie and wondered if she felt even the slightest bit the same. If she did, she hid it well.

She surprised him with the husky tone of her voice, ragged from crying, as she asked, "Did you get along with your parents?"

A moment passed as he contemplated his answer. He didn't usually share details of his family with anyone. Natalie was watching, waiting, and he gave in to the silent curiosity in her expression.

"I can't say I got along with my dad very well. He left us with nothing more than a stack of his debt when he ran off. But I guess you could say I was close to my mom."

"She died of cancer, right?"

Surprised, he nodded. "How'd you know that?"

"Mrs. Stemming told me."

A grin flashed in spite of his irritation at Gladys's big mouth. He sobered as he continued, "She died young. John was barely out of high school. I was a sophomore. It was rough but we made it work. Or, I should say, John made it work. I was just a kid, trying to get through school, impress girls and make enough money to help keep the ranch." At Natalie's subtle frown, he explained. "My dad owed a lot in back taxes, never told my mom, and when he left, the government was all set to foreclose. Every dime we had went to keeping a roof over our heads. Then Mom died and we used the small bit of life insurance that didn't go toward the funeral to fix up the ranch so we could actually start making some money, instead of constantly watch it bleed out."

"What did you guys end up doing?"

"I didn't do anything," he clarified, the admission making him feel like a giant loser, but he wasn't going to lie. "John turned the ranch into an equine clinic. He works with injured horses, gets them back on their feet, so to speak." A subtle grin tugged at his lips. "I call him the Horse Whisperer of Mariposa County. But he hates that so I wouldn't recommend it." He shifted position, giving her an intent look. "Are you going to tell me what all the waterworks are about?"

She looked unhappy again, as if she'd managed to forget, but his question brought her misery front and center. She gave her nose a short wipe and shrugged. "Thanksgiving."

"Thanksgiving?" he repeated, an awful thought coming to him. "What about it? I figured you'd spend it with your family. Don't tell me, you spent it on this sofa."

"No," she said with a sad little hiccup. "I went to my parents' house. My Aunt Jane was there," she added, though he hadn't a clue who that was or what kind of relationship she had with the woman. "But, it just wasn't the best we've ever had. Dad was civil but I can tell he's still struggling with…" She exhaled unhappily as her palm rested on her belly. She looked up at him. "Well, you know."

"He'll come around," he said, staring at the softly rounded bump without meaning to. She caught him and he gave her a small smile. "It's a lot to come to grips with. But he loves you and he'll come around. I'm sure of it."

"I wish I had your confidence," she muttered, dropping her head against the cushion. "My dad can be…a little difficult."

"Well, I don't blame him," he said, surprising her. "If some guy had knocked up my daughter, I'd be pretty pissed, too."

A contemplative expression framed her fair

features and he knew they were wondering the same thing. Did they have a daughter on the way? Would he have to worry about guys like him coming after her? His expression must've darkened because she suddenly smiled. "It takes two to tango," she reminded him.

"If that's a girl in there, there will be no tangoing in her foreseeable future until she's at least thirty," he promised her, enjoying her laughter. Her eyes lit up with amusement and chased away the sadness that had been there previously. In that moment, she reminded him so much of the way she looked in Utah that he was tempted to relive a few choice memories, such as the taste of her on his lips, the feel of her skin against his own. But it wasn't meant to be as her next question doused any amorous thoughts he might have entertained.

"So, how'd you get into rafting?"

For such an innocent question the answer had the power to kick him in the tender spots. He fell silent, searching for a way to skip past that chapter in his life without ruining the rare moment they were enjoying. His stomach growled and he jumped on the opportunity to change subjects. "I have an idea," he proposed. "Why don't you come downstairs with me. I have some chicken and veggies I was going to put into the oven. I'm sure I bought way more than I need, anyway."

Natalie appeared tempted but she shook her head. "Thanks, but I'm okay."

"You need to eat."

"I'm not hungry," she said, sighing heavily and settling more deeply into the sofa. "I'll have a protein shake later if I feel weak."

"A protein shake? I don't think so," he said, grabbing both hands and pulling her from the sofa, scattering little snotballs everywhere and making her gasp with surprise. "In case you've forgotten, you have a tendency to faint when your blood sugar gets too low. Besides," he said, with a gentle reminder, "you're eating for two."

"I know that," she said.

He tipped her chin and stared into her eyes, an unfamiliar ache blossoming in his heart when he read the uncertainty reflecting back at him. Without wasting time to think about his actions, he gathered her in his arms and she went willingly, burying her face in his chest as she huddled against his body, as if trying to absorb his strength through osmosis. He was struck by his own selfishness. Never once had he considered how difficult this must be for Natalie. He pressed a quick kiss to the top of her head and pulled her to the door, leaving little room for disagreement. "Come on, let's get that chicken going. No sense in letting good food go to waste, right?"

"I guess so," she answered reluctantly. "But only because I hate the idea of wastefulness," she added with a hint of playfulness that he found encouraging.

"Oh, of course," he said in the same tone.

She closed the door behind them, but just as his foot hit the first step, she stopped and he turned, catching the insecurity etched on her face. "Are you sure about this? I mean, won't this…complicate things?"

A dark chuckle escaped. "Natalie, I don't see how much more complicated things could get at this point. Just don't overthink it."

She nodded and he breathed a secret sigh of relief. It sounded good. Too bad it was total crap. There was something about Natalie he craved…and he was beginning to realize it really had nothing to do with the baby.

CHAPTER SIXTEEN

NATALIE SHIFTED on the exam table while her feet dangled from the edge as she awaited the nurse practitioner. There was little to do in the small room but think, so that's what she was stuck doing.

Evan.

Her parents.

The baby.

The bookstore.

A deep sigh escaped and she stretched her back. There was so much to think about and do that she hardly knew where to start. All she had were a tumult of feelings to guide her and, frankly, with all the hormones swishing around in her body, she didn't quite trust them.

The door opened and the nurse practitioner walked in with an efficient smile. "How are you feeling today?"

"A little tired and nauseous," she admitted, watching as the nurse washed her hands with sanitizer before reaching for the blood pressure cuff. She waited as the nurse took her blood pressure. When the nurse was finished Natalie added, "Actually, a lot nauseous. How long does that last?"

The nurse chuckled and returned the equipment, answering honestly. "It depends. Each woman is different. Sometimes the nausea lasts until you deliver. Other times you're lucky and it stops at the beginning of the second trimester. Let's see, how far along are you now?"

"About twenty-three weeks, I suppose," Natalie answered, watching as the nurse used the chart and a slide wheel to confirm.

"Well, if you're still sick, you might just be one of those fortunate women who get to enjoy a sensitive stomach until the baby arrives. Do you have any help at home? Someone who can prepare meals so you don't have to worry about smells bothering you?"

Evan flew to mind with a speed that was almost unnatural and she frowned at the direction of her own thoughts. She shook her head. "It's not that bad. I know what to stay away from."

"All right," the nurse said with another benign smile. "Let's check out that heartbeat."

Natalie beamed with genuine pleasure. This was her favorite part. She scooted back on the small table and lifted her top to expose the small, rounded bump her belly had become. The nurse squeezed some warm goo on her stomach and put the Doppler wand to her skin. At first there was nothing but static, then suddenly, as if emerging from underwater, a fast staccato rhythm sounded in the room and immediately tears jumped to her eyes. "Ohhh," she breathed, looking at the nurse with wonder. "It's so fast. Is that normal?"

The nurse grinned. "Perfectly. Sounds like a strong heart to me," she said, removing the Doppler and wiping it clean. She handed Natalie a towel to clean herself. "It's about time for your first ultrasound. I like to do the first one around sixteen to twenty-two weeks and you're already past that mark."

A thrill chased the realization she was going to catch the first glimpse of her child. "Can you tell the sex of the baby?"

"Usually, but I wouldn't get your hopes up

right away. Babies can be notoriously shy at just the right moment. But if you want to know we'll see what we can do. Now, are there any other questions?"

Natalie chewed her lip then asked if she could bring anyone with her.

"Of course. But the room is small so no more than one person. We can put it on a DVD though if you'd like—that way you can share it with the whole family."

With that, the nurse told her she'd see her next month, assuming there were no problems, and gave instructions for her to make an appointment at the front desk for the ultrasound.

Natalie grabbed her purse and let herself out, her mind moving in foreign directions. Should she invite Evan to come? Would that complicate matters even more than they already were?

She approached the desk, still conflicted. A part of her really wanted him there, but she wasn't sure how to approach him or how he'd react.

"I have an opening in two weeks. How's two p.m.?"

Natalie nodded, breathing out silently.

She had two weeks to figure out whether or not it was wise to invite Evan to the ultrasound. Hopefully, it was enough time to sort things out.

EVAN TURNED the corner and easily found Natalie's bookstore, right where he was told it would be, sandwiched between an old-fashioned ice-cream parlor and a florist.

Two wide windows graced the front, allowing Evan a clear view of Natalie perched on a ladder with a paintbrush in her hand. Her movements were a little awkward when she bent down to dip her brush into the paint can, as her belly was beginning to poke out a bit. A wondrous smile started to form at the pronounced evidence of her pregnancy until he realized with a horrified start that she was wobbling on the ladder.

"What the hell are you doing?" he asked, moving quickly to steady the ladder before she toppled in a painted mess on the canvas-covered floor. "Are you nuts? You shouldn't be on a ladder. Get down, right now."

At his commanding tone Natalie stiffened and her jaw hardened. "I was fine and I will not get down. I have work to do." She turned as if dismissing him, but he wasn't about to be dismissed so easily and gently gripped her by the waist and pulled her down. "Hey! What are you doing?" she demanded.

His hands still around her waist and feeling quite comfortable there, he replied with an arched brow, "You ask a lot of questions with answers that are pretty obvious, you know that?"

"And you assume a lot," she retorted with a pointed look at his hands, forcing him to reluctantly relinquish his hold.

He crossed his arms and met her scowl with one of his own. "What would have happened if you'd fallen?"

"Well, I didn't fall," she said defensively. "And that was the first time that has ever happened. Usually, the ladder is quite steady."

Evan pressed his lips together, wondering how to attack this particular argument without sparking a heated exchange. He didn't want to fight with her but he wanted her to stop taking chances. He stepped back and let his gaze roam the work in progress. "Not bad. I like the fantasy theme. Did you paint the murals?" he said, offering a silent truce.

A wary but proud smile followed as she nodded, not quite sure what to make of his sudden change in attitude. "It's just fancy doodling really, but I think it turned out pretty good."

More than just *pretty good*, he thought, impressed. His gaze traced the intricate scrollwork that dipped and meandered the edging toward the ceiling. The wall was texturized to look like parchment, lending an old-world feel to the whole room.

"This is the last wall that needs paint before I can start the dragon mural."

"A dragon mural? Sounds complicated."

"Not really. I've already sketched it out. Want to see?"

"Sure." If she considered the murals on the walls doodling, what would she call true artwork, he wondered. Her enthusiastic smile lit up her face as she went to a large binder full of loose paper and he trailed after her, the subtle scent of vanilla crooking a finger in his direction and practically pulling him along. Settling behind her, he tried to keep a respectable distance between them, but it was hard keeping his body from leaning in her general direction. Natalie was too busy flipping through her sketchpad to notice his struggle, or his close proximity. She smelled good enough to eat. Like a cookie or something. A nicely rounded, sexy cookie. She found the one she was searching for and turned, almost running in to him. She gave him a strange look and he took a step back so she could hand him the sketch.

The dragon, sketched in pencil, was imperious and fierce, definitely not something he'd expect to see in a children's bookstore, but he immediately liked it. He looked up. Natalie's expression was endearingly anxious as she awaited his opinion. The very fact that she cared what he thought caused his chest to fill with something unlike he'd ever known. It was foreign but it didn't feel wrong. He met her gaze. "I love it," he said simply. "It's the best I've ever seen. And this is definitely more than just doodling. Doodling typically involves stick people in various poses…not detailed dragon portraits. It's fantastic."

"Thanks," she said, her hands fluttering to her stomach and drawing his attention. He itched to feel that round bump in his palms, to know as it grew each month, instead of catching what felt like stolen glimpses.

She darted a look at him. "So…what are you doing here?"

He smiled as he answered, "I'm here to help. No more climbing ladders or wielding heavy machinery for you. Not while I'm around. So, where do I start?"

Her expression faltered and her mouth fell open to protest, but when Evan made it apparent he wasn't going to back down, she slapped a paintbrush in his hand and pointed toward the far wall. "Fine. I need that whole wall painted in this color for the base. When you're done there, you can start on the texturizing."

"What are you going to be doing?" he asked, watching her warily.

"I'll be putting some finishing touches on the faerie mural, no ladders needed. Is that all right with you, Mr. Paranoid?"

A grudging smile lifted the corner of his mouth and he grabbed a paintcan. "Glad to see we're both on the same page." *Finally.*

They settled into an amiable silence, working on their individual projects, but Evan could almost feel the sidelong glances coming his way. Without music or background noise to fill the space between them, he knew the questions would start. In his experience, a woman rarely let silence run its course. He wasn't disappointed.

"So…why didn't you stay at the ranch with your brother?"

Evan sighed, knowing conversation of this sort was inevitable. She was having his kid, it was only natural to want to know something about the father, right? Yeah. Logic was one thing…wanting to cooperate was another. But, when he turned she was watching him intently and there was no getting out of it without ruining the pleasant afternoon. "Ranch work's not really my thing," he admitted, stopping only long enough to dip his brush and continue painting. At least if he was occupied, maybe she wouldn't feel compelled to delve too deeply. The silence following his statement weighed on him and he found himself adding reluctantly, "Plus, John made it possible for me to go to college. He said one of us needed to be educated so that no one could ever try and take the ranch again."

"Oh, wow. That was really cool of your brother."

"Yeah. He's a good guy," he said. "He's done a lot for me."

"But, you didn't go back to the ranch... you went into river-rafting?"

"Like I said...ranching was never my thing. Besides, John's never really needed my degree. He does fine on his own and whatever he can't figure out, he's got Steve to help him through."

"Who's Steve?"

"Business manager."

Again, that "oh" and Evan wondered if she was judging him. "He does fine. Really. I wouldn't leave my brother to fend for himself after everything he's done for me."

"I know you wouldn't."

He glanced up and caught her expression. She believed in him. It felt good but a small part of him didn't feel deserving of her support. For a while he *had* abandoned John. After Hailey, he pretty much abandoned everything. Selfish, yes, but he'd thought he was going to lose his mind.

"Evan?" Her voice softened and uncertainty returned to her gaze. When he looked at her questioningly, she bit her lip, then continued with a hastily drawn breath as if she needed courage. "I found an independent lab that does paternity tests. Do you still want one done?"

He stared at her. His heart said no, his head said yes. Legally, he'd need that slip of paper if he planned to push for joint custody. He nodded reluctantly and even felt compelled to apologize. "I believe it's my child but I have to protect my rights. I mean, everything is going okay between us right now but, I'd rather—"

"I can have it done next week," she interrupted. The expression on her face sliced into him, but he saw no way around it unless they planned to get married right away. "Is that soon enough?"

"That's fine. Thank you," he added.

She rewarded him with a tight smile and they returned to their painting. A few moments later, she exhaled loudly and turned back to him. "I have another question," she said.

"Which is?"

"Would you like to go to the sonogram with me next Friday?"

NATALIE HELD HER BREATH. There. She said it. Biting her lip against the wild thumping of her heart, she willed him to say the right thing. Except, he didn't say anything. He just stared…and his expression wavered on the verge of fear. That was hardly encouraging.

She frowned. "Never mind—" she started brusquely, turning to the wall. What was she thinking? "I just thought—"

"You thought right," he said, and she turned quickly, catching the subtle change in his expression. "I'm just surprised you asked."

"Why?" It wasn't a fair question but she wanted to know his answer just the same.

"Because things aren't what you'd call ideal between us. I mean, we aren't even a couple but we're having a baby. I didn't think I'd get to be a part of those prebirth privileges, if you know what I mean."

She did and had the grace to feel bad that he felt excluded. "I'm not trying to keep you from the baby," she said softly. "I just want what's best. You understand, right?" *For me, too.*

Evan looked away and a long pause followed. His jaw, strong as it was stubborn, was sprinkled with a day's growth of golden stubble, giving him a rakish appearance that was almost too cute for words. For a moment Natalie was lost to the fact that he still hadn't answered. But once she came her to her senses, she tried again. "Evan?" she asked. Her worried tone drew his attention and he surprised her with a slow grin.

"Let's call it a night," he suggested, wiping his forearm across his brow then reaching down to collect the soiled brushes. "It's not like we have to solve everything this minute."

Disappointment stole her urge to return the smile. Her first impression of Evan had been of a happy-go-lucky guy, but she'd long ago realized that there was so much more to the man and it was his reluctance to share that made her nervous. She turned away. "You go ahead. I'm not quite ready to stop yet."

"Natalie, don't be so stubborn. You're exhausted."

That's the pot calling the kettle black, she thought darkly. He was the one who kept avoiding the big issues. It's not like they had all the time in the world to figure these things out. She purposefully dabbed her brush and returned to her mural. "Could you lock the door on your way out?" she said with her back to him, anger at the situation replacing any warm and fuzzy feelings she'd had earlier.

"You're being ridiculous. C'mon, we can come back tomorrow."

She turned only long enough to send him a pointed stare. "There's still so much to do and I already lost too much time when I was down with morning sickness. You're welcome to go but I'm staying."

"You have dark circles under your eyes and your arm is shaking."

Damn. He wasn't supposed to see that. "Well, I'm out of shape. You try holding your arm in one place for hours at a stretch," she retorted defensively, rotating her shoulder against the burning muscles. "Besides, I have a deadline. The opening is in two months and I still have two murals to paint, inventory to put on shelves and finish the décor. There's so much…I don't have time to rest." *Don't forget, I have to give birth shortly after,* she wanted to add but didn't. That point was obvious.

"I'll make you a deal," he said, garnering her faint interest. "Let's go home tonight, get something to eat and tomorrow we'll return at the crack of dawn. I'll be at your beck and call, I promise. With the two of us working, we should be able to make up your lost time. Sound good?"

Oh, the temptation. Who was she kidding? If she didn't drop from fatigue in about two minutes, it'd be a miracle. She relented. "All right," she said, her drooping eyelids giving her away as much as the yawn that followed. "I probably wouldn't be able to get much done anyway," she grudgingly admitted. "Let's close up."

They made short work of cleaning the brushes and putting away the supplies for the night, and within thirty minutes she was locking up and heading to her car.

As Natalie fumbled with her keys, cursing her clumsy fingers as she almost dropped them for the second time, she heard Evan call out to her from his truck. If she wasn't mistaken there was a hint of laughter in his voice. She turned and scowled. "What?"

"You look like you're having some trouble," he said, leaning against the door-frame as if he didn't have a care in the world. "Do you want a ride?"

Sure. Can I sit on your lap? "No. I'm fine. Go ahead." She slid the right key in the door and gratefully ducked inside, resisting the urge to cast a look his way. Evan might not feel it was necessary to have things ironed out just yet but Natalie disagreed. It seems they disagreed a lot. Was that how they would be when the baby arrived? She hated the idea of constantly bickering, especially when all she really wanted to do was pretend that nothing between them was strained and that they truly were a family. What a stupid yearning, she mused the moment the forbidden thought crossed her mind. An unhappy sigh followed and she pulled out to the street. A girl could wish, couldn't she?

EVAN GAVE NATALIE a full three-minute head start, his mind moving quickly in erratic circles. There was so much to work out. Custody, visitation, support. The thought of taking the baby from Natalie even for a weekend seemed wrong, but he couldn't imagine being away from his child, either. That only left one option and, surprisingly, it didn't fill him with distaste. Something about Natalie twisted and curled past his defenses and teased him with the promise of a warm and wonderful future that he'd only dreamed about since Hailey. *But what future would that be?* He frowned at the harsh voice cutting into his thoughts and realized he didn't have an answer. Driving into his parking slot, he killed the ignition and pulled the key out as he slowly leaned against the headrest. Was he really ready to be a father?

If he tore away the pride and the emotional baggage he was still lugging around from the past, he had to acknowledge that one simple truth. He'd spent the last ten years living like a man in his early twenties, day by day, without a care to where he'd be next, and there'd been a certain pleasure to his bohemian lifestyle. But it certainly wasn't a lifestyle he'd drag a child into and therein lay the problem. He was hell-bent on being in this child's life, but what did that mean for his own? He couldn't expect Natalie to shoulder the brunt of the financial burden, but he was hardly rolling in cash. He had some in savings but if he didn't go replenish in the winter what he was spending now, his reserve would disappear. Hell, he might just have to put that fancy piece of paper, as John called it, to good use...and get a real job. But, he thought with a sliver of uncertainty, what was out there for him to do?

CHAPTER SEVENTEEN

NATALIE PLUCKED at the front of her blouse, trying to hide her burgeoning bump, but it was no use, her belly was getting out there and she wasn't even six months yet.

"I think I'm going to give birth to a sumo wrestler," she grumbled to Nora, who was busy enjoying a Cobb salad as if she were starved. "Look at me. I'm already huge."

"No, you're not. You're pregnant." Nora's answer wasn't reassuring—that's what everyone said to pregnant women even if they were big enough to block the sun. Natalie gave her sister a look communicating that fact and Nora grinned as if she'd been caught. "Okay. You're huge. Is that what you want to hear?" Nora laughed at Natalie's outraged gasp, continuing without missing a beat, "I'm just kidding. You're not huge. Why all the paranoia? You've never been one to obsess about your weight. Of all the times, I'd think now would be the perfect time to just enjoy eating whatever your body wants. After all, you can always blame it on the baby, right?"

Easy enough for Nora to say. She didn't have to pack around the extra forty pounds. Natalie's back was already starting to twinge every now and then. Besides, she didn't want to look huge. There was nothing sexy about swollen ankles and the fine layer of fuzz starting to sprout all over her body from the overactive hormones zinging through her body and playing Ping-Pong with the functioning area of her brain. "I feel frumpy," she grumbled nonetheless, adding under her breath, "and ugly."

"Are you looking to date?"

"No," she said too quickly, earning an amused look from Nora as she resumed eating her salad. "No, it's not like that… really. I'm just unaccustomed to losing control of my body like this. That's all. I mean, how attractive would you feel if you started ballooning like I am?"

Nora laughed. "Not very. But, like I said… you're pregnant. You'll drop the weight after you have the baby. Don't worry."

"I'm not." Her voice rose a notch.

"Good. Besides, I've read that some guys think pregnant women are really sexy."

"Where'd you read that?" Natalie asked, her thoughts immediately moving to Evan and how he might feel about her growing status.

Nora shrugged. "I can't remember. But it's true. You should see how Mike Zibowski gets all gooey-eyed when he looks at Sharon. She's gotta be at least nine months by now and I'd wager she's gained her fair share of weight. You'd never know it to see how Mike looks at her."

Natalie's spirits sank. "Nora, she's his wife. Of course, he's going to look at her like that. He loves her." She could hardly expect Evan, or anyone else for that matter, to look at her that way when they didn't share the same kind of bond. Not that she wouldn't mind Evan looking at her like that, she realized privately. He was, after all, the father of her child.

"You're starting to like the guy, aren't you?" Nora said suddenly, causing Natalie to jump guiltily. Nora laughed at her reaction. She started to stammer a denial but Nora wasn't buying. "No, I think you have feelings for Evan, except now you're getting big and pregnant and you're afraid he's not going to be attracted to you. Don't you think it's ironic that you'd want to seduce the man who got you pregnant in the first place?"

"I'm not trying to seduce him," she said indignantly. "I just don't like being so... ungainly."

"Right."

Nora's dry answer had her wondering if she was truly transparent or if Nora just knew her well enough to guess what was going through her head. She hoped it was the latter. She could deal with Nora reading her mind; but if Evan had an inkling of the unwelcome feelings curling through her body every time they were around each other she'd die of embarrassment.

"Let's change the subject," she suggested, drawing a deep breath as she broached the subject that brought about the invitation to lunch in the first place. "I asked Evan to go with me to my first sonogram."

"Really?" Nora said in surprise, her eyes wide but encouraging. "That's very generous of you. Why the change of heart?"

She wasn't sure. Hormones were probably

partly to blame, except Natalie wasn't quite ready to delve that deeply into her motivation. "He's been a big help down at the store," she said, shrugging, "and, I don't know, I thought he might enjoy it."

"I'm sure he will," Nora agreed. "Are you sure that's all there is to it?"

"What else could there be? We're not even a couple," she said, repeating Evan's statement.

"I bet you could change his mind on that score," Nora said confidently.

"I'm not saying that I would want to…but what makes you think so?" She gave her sister a sidelong glance, wondering what Nora saw that she obviously did not.

She shrugged. "A hunch."

Natalie drew back. *A hunch.* She wasn't about to chance humiliating herself on a hunch. "Well, we're not very compatible so it's a moot point." Gearing up for a rebuttal, she was oddly disappointed when Nora seemed to agree. "Do you think we're incompatible?" she asked, unable to stop herself.

"Who cares what I think? All that matters is what you think. You're the only one who knows how you feel," Nora answered.

A groan escaped as she placed her head in her hands. She wished it were that simple. Lately, she didn't know which end was up when it came to the way she felt. All she knew was the longer she was around Evan, the harder it became to stay away.

"I saw Dan the other day," Nora said, switching subjects. "I heard he got dumped. He was asking about you."

"What'd you say?" Natalie asked, lifting her head to stare at her sister warily.

A devilish grin tugged at her sister's lips and trepidation filled Natalie's chest. "I told him you were six months pregnant from a one-night stand but would love it if he gave you a call."

"You didn't!"

Nora blinked with the beguiling innocence befitting a Disney character. "And what if I did? I thought your heart belonged to Dan."

Blech. "Please tell me you're joking."

Nora broke out into a peal of laughter. "I'm kidding. But he did ask about you. I said you were doing well and completely in love with this hot guy you met while rafting. The look on his dumb face was priceless!"

Natalie laughed and it felt good. Thoughts of Dan no longer brought a sharp pain to her chest. Neither did news that he was single again tempt her to give him a call. Thankfully, they hadn't bumped into each other yet despite the relative small quarters of Emmett's Mill. Natalie may be over him but she certainly didn't want him to see her pregnant and alone. She had her pride.

"So, have you had the paternity test done yet?"

"Not yet. I was hoping he would change his mind."

Nora looked at her. "And I'm taking it he didn't change his mind?"

Natalie shook her head. "Nope."

"So, he doesn't believe you?"

"Oh, it's not that. I almost wish that's all it was. No, he needs it for legal purposes because we're not married or a couple."

"How pragmatic of him," Nora said between another mouthful of salad, then continued on another note. "Hmm…well, you are a deplorable liar. Besides, you hardly give off that 'insatiable sex fiend' vibe. If you got pregnant in anything other than the missionary position, I'll eat my own shoe."

"How about I just put my shoe up your butt instead," Natalie retorted.

"Someone's sensitive." Nora laughed and tossed a small piece of ice at Natalie, causing her to smile even as she dodged. When she straightened, and Nora was certain retaliation was not immediately forthcoming, she asked if Natalie thought there was anything happening between them.

"Aside from the fact that we made a baby together?"

"Yeah, besides that. You know, like any kind of emotional stuff. Personally, I think he has feelings for you. I think he has since the minute he came to return your necklace."

"And where do you get this information? Another hunch?" Natalie asked, her tone dubious.

Nora grinned. "You got it. I'm pretty intuitive about things like that."

Natalie rolled her eyes. "Oh, great. Nora the love doctor is in."

"Laugh if you want but I'll bet you twenty bucks he's thinking of you in ways that aren't PG-13. My guess is…he wants to see you naked!"

"Get real. I'm as big as a house and guaranteed to get even bigger. That's not very attractive. The other day I tried to put on a pair of my old underwear and they barely fit over my hips."

"Well, that's what you get for trying to wear a thong when you're in your second trimester."

Natalie smiled, almost guiltily. It had been a thong. And she was thankful she'd been all alone in her bedroom because she looked pretty darn ridiculous squeezed into that scrap of material. It was probably stretched into oblivion. An elephant could no doubt wear it as a headband at this point.

Although Natalie scoffed at Nora's implication that she and Evan might ever have a future beyond custody exchanges, a secret part of her hoped such a thing was possible despite the knowledge that Evan wasn't the sort to settle down and get a nine-to-five job. What was she thinking? Even if Evan harbored similar feelings, Natalie wasn't about to let her heart get tangled up with a man who was gone most of the time. Her baby deserved more.

Nora cut into her thoughts and she was grateful for the interruption. "Do you still need me down at the bookstore?" she asked, pausing before taking a final bite. "If so, when?"

Natalie bit her lip in thought. Now that

Evan was helping her, the work was coming along at a nice clip. The walls were completely painted and Natalie was ready to start the dragon mural. "Soon," she promised. "Just keep your schedule open within the next two weeks."

"Will do," Nora answered, eyeing Natalie's almost untouched lunch with a frown. "You're going to eat that, aren't you?"

"What?" Natalie asked, distracted by the ongoing list in her head of things the bookstore needed to have done before she could open. Nora pointed at her turkey sandwich with an arched brow. "Oh, yes, later maybe. I'll get a to-go box. I have to get back to the bookstore and start on the mural before Evan gets there or else he'll freak out when he sees me on the ladder again."

"You're climbing ladders?" Nora asked, incredulous. "Are you nuts? You're way too pregnant. Your center of balance is going to be off."

"Well, I'm the only one who can draw the dragon and it's essential it's done right. It's my centerpiece. I mean, I can't have a bookstore called The Dragon's Lair without a pretty cool dragon, right?"

"I guess, but can't you get someone else to do it?" Nora asked.

"No," Natalie answered decidedly. "It has to be me. But don't worry. I'll be fine. I promise."

NATALIE LEANED BACK and surveyed her work, careful not to lean too far as she balanced her weight on the ladder. She grinned despite the ache in her back. It was turning out exceptionally well and she couldn't help but feel proud. Her dream was finally taking shape.

Climbing down carefully, she wrangled the ladder to a new position and resumed her perch with a paintbrush clenched between her teeth as she readied her palette. The door jingled and Natalie was startled to see her father standing in the doorway, his expression darkening as he spotted her.

"Don't you think you ought to get down from there considering your condition?"

Not about to ruin the moment with an argument about how capable she was, she climbed down with a tentative smile. "Hello, Daddy. What do you think of my shop?"

Shoving his hands into his front pockets he gave the unfinished store a once-over, finishing with a noncommittal nod of his head that Natalie took as a good sign, even if it was up to interpretation. He eyed the mural as if it were the enemy and Natalie's spirits faltered. "It's not done yet," she said, defending her work. "But when it's finished I think it'll be fantastic."

"Don't you have any help? Where's Nora?" He gazed up at the dragon again, his mouth pursing. "What about the father? Why isn't he around helping out?"

The spit dried in Natalie's mouth—she was unsure of how to defend Evan without giving away too much. She wasn't ready to involve her parents with her current situation. They would never understand the complicated nature of her relationship with Evan. To them, it was cut and dried. If he was the father, it was his duty to marry her. Natalie winced at the very thought of being dragged to the altar with a shotgun leveled at Evan's chest should he balk. Her father wasn't *that* old-school, but lately, his fuse was shorter than usual and she didn't want to risk it.

"Well?" her father prompted gruffly, drawing her back to the present as she searched for the best way to answer a difficult question. The lengthy pause wore on her father's patience and he snorted in disgust. "Never mind. It's apparent whoever this guy is that got you pregnant isn't much of a man at all in my book. Otherwise, he'd be here. Where it counts."

Guilt weighed on her conscience but cowardice held her tongue. What difference did it make what her father thought of Evan? It wasn't as if they were going to sit across the table from one another during holiday get-togethers. Once they figured out custody exchanges, she doubted Evan and her father's paths would ever cross. Her spirits sank at her own logic but before she had time to examine her reasons, her father had moved to the door and she quickly followed.

"Daddy…you didn't say—what do you think of the store so far?" she asked, tears threatening to spill as she waited for his approval. "It's good, right?"

Natalie held her breath as her father gave the store another stern once-over, his gaze seeming to stop on every unfinished detail until she was ready to pass out from the pounding of her heart. Then, just when she thought she couldn't take it anymore, his expression softened and he gave a short nod. "Looking good, so far," he said, to her immense relief. But as she drew a deep breath, he pointed a stubbed finger at the ladder and made her promise she'd stay off it unless Nora was here to help. "You're too far along to be taking chances like that," he pointed out.

"All right, Daddy. I'll wait for Nora," she promised.

Gerald took a cursory walk around the shop, poking his nose down aisles, noting the work in progress, but Natalie could sense his interest wasn't entirely true. There was something else behind his stare. "Daddy?" she asked, concerned. "What's wrong?"

He stopped and finally shook his head before coming to stand before the large front window. "There's something I need to say and it's not going to be easy," he began, his lips tightening as if a part of him was attempting to trap the words before they tumbled out of his mouth. He sent a glance her way to gauge her reaction, then back out toward the street. "I might've been wrong to react the way I did when you told me about the baby."

Natalie withheld the gasp of surprise that

followed his admission, hardly able to believe she was witnessing an apology from her father. "It's okay, Dad—"

"No, it's not," he acknowledged gruffly, facing her. "Babies come when they come and you're going to be a great mother."

"You think so?"

"I know so." He drew a deep breath and his mouth crooked in a wry manner that reminded her so much of Nora that she almost chuckled at the irony. "Besides," he continued with more emotion than she'd ever seen, "your mom is right, you're going to need your family through this and I'm not going to be the one to chase you away."

Tasha. Her sister's crushed expression floated out of her memory and she knew without having to say it aloud they were both thinking of her and the night she left.

"Thank you, Daddy," she whispered, knowing how deep that particular scar went and how much it cost him to come to her like this.

A stiff nod followed and no more words were needed. He gave one last look around the store, the approval in his shrewd gaze speaking volumes to her heart, and walked out the door.

Anyone who didn't know her father like she did wouldn't think much of his visit, but she knew it took a huge concession on his part to come down and she was overcome with relief. The only part about the visit that rubbed her wrong was his judgment on Evan. He wasn't the bad guy her father assumed he was, but Natalie hadn't been ready to defend him for selfish reasons and now she couldn't shake a residual queasiness.

Get over it. Evan and her father were never going to meet so what difference did it make? She shrugged off her concerns and readjusted her ladder. She considered closing up for the day and coming back tomorrow, when Nora said she could lend a hand, but she was so close to attaining her goal and the mural beckoned. She ascended the ladder carefully, mindful of her belly, and grabbed her palette. Finishing the dragon mural was priority number one and so far she was making good progress on her list of details that needed finishing before she could open. She smiled, feeling decidedly lighter inside after her father's visit, and started to paint. Maybe things weren't so bleak after all.

CHAPTER EIGHTEEN

EVAN PULLED UP to the ranch amid a cloud of dust and climbed out, waving at John in the arena as he worked with a painted mare with a bandaged left back leg. John paused long enough to give him a speculative look, but the mare demanded his attention before long and Evan was no longer his main concern.

Taking the front porch steps two at a time, he walked into the ranch house that he'd grown up in and the familiar smells enveloped him like a warm embrace. This house belonged to him and John, but it would always remain his mother's house unless John got married someday and brought a woman home to make it her own. Until then, it would always retain their mother's spirit in the starched doilies on the antique buffet and the polished wood floors that shone despite their age. John, orderly by nature, kept the house neat as a pin. At least any woman John happened to bring home wouldn't find cause to complain about a messy bachelor pad. John was the only unmarried man who lived like he had a wife tucked away somewhere. He chuckled at his own thoughts and headed for the attic. He'd come for something specific.

Below, toward the front of the house, the screen door banged and footsteps followed as John called out his name.

"Up here," he answered, pulling cobwebs away from his face as he searched for the item he'd come for. "In the attic." A shaft of yellow light filtered in from the one small window and once his eyes adjusted to the dark corners, his search ended and a pleased smile curved his mouth. His mother's rocker, handcrafted as a gift by his maternal grandfather when she'd married his dad, it was made from solid oak and would probably outlast them all. He figured it wasn't doing anyone any good in a dusty attic, but Natalie could sure use it once the baby arrived. Careful not to damage it, he gently pulled it from its resting place and made his way gingerly down the attic steps with it placed precariously on his shoulders.

"What do you think you're doing?"

His brother's stern voice surprised him and he twisted. "What does it look like? Give me a hand, will ya?"

A scowl darkened John's face but he reached out to accept the rocking chair so Evan could climb down without falling or breaking the chair. Once he was down he offered a quick thanks and reached for it, but John's grip tightened. "Where do you think you're taking Momma's rocking chair?"

Suddenly indignant, Evan placed his hands on his hips. "You're not using it. What difference does it make?"

"It makes a whole helluva lot of difference cuz you're not taking it outta this house unless you tell me where it's going."

Evan opened his mouth to fire off another angry statement but he realized he wasn't being fair to John. Since he'd come home they'd done nothing but exchange terse words all because Evan was struggling with himself, and wasn't quite sure where his place was in the world anymore. He wasn't a kid but he didn't feel like a man, either. John had always been good to him, probably the best older brother a guy could ask for.

The least he could do is level with him. Straightening, he said, "You know that girl I told you about? Well, I thought she might be able to put it to good use." He shrugged a bit sheepishly, thinking he probably should've cleared his decision with John first. "Actually, I was thinking of giving it to her for Christmas as an heirloom for our son or daughter. But…if you're not cool with that…"

John waved away his question. "It's fine. You're right. It should be put to use rather than collect dust in the attic," he said. He continued with a speculative look. "So, you're really going to be a father? No joke?"

"No joke. You're going to be an uncle. Scary thought, that," he added with a small grin.

John's expression faltered as the implication sunk in and he actually paled under his tan. Inhaling deeply, he eyed Evan seriously. "I don't know what to say except to ask are you happy?"

Evan took a moment to consider his answer, then nodded. "Yeah, I am."

"Is that why you moved up there?"

He nodded again. "Yeah, I took an apartment directly below hers so I could be nearby if she needed anything." That and he was terrified if he wasn't around she'd go and do something drastic like start contacting adoption agencies. "She's something else. I think you'd like her. Gladys loved her."

"Gladys? As in our neighbor?"

"The very same. They met on the rafting trip and really hit it off."

"Oh, man, so does Gladys know that your girl is pregnant?" he asked, wide-eyed.

"I told her at the Thanksgiving party. And by the way, who is this Anna Morgan woman you were tripping all over yourself to be near?"

John opened his mouth and his ears reddened before he answered gruffly, "None of your damn business and don't change the subject."

Evan laughed. "Looks like I've hit a tender spot. When do I get to meet her?"

The flustered expression on his brother's face was priceless. If he'd had a camera, he'd have gleefully captured it for all eternity. "Let me guess, you haven't told her how you feel?" he said, receiving a dark look for an answer.

"What about you? You told your woman how you feel about her?"

"She's not my woman. She's just carrying my child," he corrected, though he had to admit that sounded a little odd. But he was having too much fun at the moment to go into detail about his relationship with Natalie. "Now, who's changing the subject?" he taunted with a teasing grin.

"Anna's just a friend," John finally muttered, hooking his thumbs in his belt loops. "She likes horses."

"Convenient."

"Aw, shut up."

Evan laughed and hoisted the rocker, moving past John and into the kitchen where he could smell coffee brewing.

"So, what's the deal with you two?" John asked, as he followed Evan into the kitchen.

"It's complicated," Evan answered, grabbing two mugs from the cabinet and pouring each of them a full cup of the black brew that Evan knew from experience would be strong enough to make his hair stand on end. He took a bracing sip and grimaced.

"It always is," his brother retorted, following suit without so much as a blink. "You love this woman?" he asked, once again the big brother and in control of the conversation.

Evan stopped, his cup midway to his mouth, and exhaled as he lifted his shoulder. "Not sure. Maybe. Like I said, it's complicated."

"I bet once you figure out your feelings it'll become a lot less complicated," John advised, taking another sip.

"She makes me feel things I haven't felt since Hailey and that freaks me out more than a bit," he said, setting down his mug and straightening to stare out the window toward the arena. "And, honestly, I don't even know if I *want* to feel those things."

"Are they anything alike?"

John's blunt question burned and he mentally flinched at the truth staring back at him. Shaking his head, he answered, "I thought so for a while, but now I don't know. I thought I knew Hailey and look how well that turned out."

"True." John finished his coffee and rinsed it out in the sink, putting the mug on the drainer to dry. He turned to Evan, crossing his arms. "But she's not Hailey and you're not the same dumb kid you were ten years ago. If you love her, give her a chance. You might not get another."

Evan stared at his brother, sensing there

was a layer of something personal behind his statement that John kept protected under lock and key. Evan shifted on the balls of his feet, tempted to venture into that area, which was clearly marked "off-limits," but John removed the opportunity by striding toward the front door. Just as he walked out, he tossed a final comment over his shoulder. "Make sure you tie that thing down real good. If you break it, I'll break your head. And," he added for good measure, "Anna's just a friend. No matter what Gladys thinks or says."

Hard-ass, Evan thought, a smile full of respect nudging his lips. But that was his brother. He'd probably never change. And Evan hoped to God he never did. John was the one thing in his life that remained stable—no matter what he did to screw it up.

THE DAY WAS LATE and fire burned down her arm as she dabbed paint into the intricate scales of the dragon's massive body, but Natalie was intent on finishing the mural. She was almost there. *So close.* A giddy smile, weary around the edges, formed as she adjusted her body on the ladder. Her back had gone from mildly protesting to screaming its displeasure and her right leg had gone almost numb from the pressure she was exerting to keep herself from falling. But the dragon was magnificent, she thought, fierce pride strengthening her body from within.

For the first time in her life she was moving in a direction of her choosing and even though it was frightening to head into the unknown, the freedom was liberating. Little snatches of an annoying pop song came to her head and she started humming as she continued to work. She could almost see the scores of kids pouring into her bookstore, clamoring for the newest Harry Potter book, begging their parents for just a few more minutes as they devoured the pages of their favorite story from the cocoon of a comfy reading chair, something soft and squishy and fire-engine red, she decided with a tired giggle. She paused, noting the quickly descending sun in the horizon and the chill in the air as winter made its presence known. The storefronts on the main street featured brightly colored lights for the holiday season and Natalie sighed as she realized how quickly time was moving. Soon, she and Evan would be parents. Sobering, she worried her bottom lip as reality descended with the weight of an elephant. There was a grain of truth to Nora's earlier statement that despite her best efforts, she was falling for a man who, by all appearances, was allergic to commitment. If she was apprehensive over Evan's role as a father, what possible role could she expect him to play with her?

Her pride kept her from admitting the fears or desires that plagued her dreams. She was afraid if she opened her heart she'd get nothing but rejection in those beautiful eyes, when she yearned to see them soften with affection and more.

Enough, she told herself sternly. She had bigger things to worry about than the status of her love life. Such as finishing this dragon…

As she surveyed her work, she noted a small spot needing a second coat and, after daubing her brush into the color needed, she stretched on her tiptoes to reach it. She was nearly finished when a vicious cramp started from the center of her arch and traveled to her calf, feeling as if the muscle was shredding as it pulled and twisted. Clutching at her calf, a shriek followed her short sob as the pain intensified and she lost her balance. Within a blink she was falling and then she connected with the hardwood floor—and everything went black.

EVAN WHISTLED as he walked the short distance from his truck to the bookstore, not even the slightest bit surprised that Natalie's car was still parked outside. It was nearing six o'clock, but one thing he'd learned about Natalie was that she didn't stop until she'd met her own personal quota for the day. He appreciated her work ethic, though it reminded him of himself in his younger days, and that brought up conflicting feelings. Still, after spending the day at the ranch he felt more centered than he had in months. John's statement had made him think and he was cautiously enjoying his decision to stop judging Natalie by the actions of another. It seemed a simple thing but Evan knew it wouldn't be easy. He had years of mental conditioning to contend with and he didn't suspect the walls he'd spent ten years building would crumble so easily. Yet when he pictured Natalie's face, warmth suffused his body and he couldn't stop the smile that immediately followed. That had to account for something, right? He figured so, and he was willing to test the theory.

As he approached the bookstore, his gaze immediately sought out the familiar figure that, despite the growing silhouette was becoming a regular feature in his more erotic dreams. A smile curved his mouth as he privately enjoyed the mental imagery, until he pushed open the front door and saw Natalie lying on the floor, a large bloodstain beneath her.

"Natalie!" he roared, fear, shock and horror galvanizing him into action. "Oh, God, what happened?" he asked, though he knew no answer would come from her unconscious form. He fought the urge to cradle her against his chest and instead jerked his cell phone from his jean pocket to dial 911 with shaking fingers.

"What is the nature of your emergency?"

"I need an ambulance right away!"

"Sir, hold on a moment, can you tell me who's hurt?"

Evan stuttered, raking a hand through his hair. What was he supposed to say? The woman he managed to knock up on a one-night stand? He couldn't say that, but neither could he say they were friends. They were in a state of limbo but that didn't help the 911 operator at the moment. Evan's gaze strayed to Natalie's inert body and his hand curled around the phone. *Screw it.*

"Sir?"

"It's my wife," he answered quickly, knowing his mother would forgive him this whopper of a white lie if she happened to be watching his actions from above. "And she's pregnant. She's fallen and there's blood...oh, God, there's lots of blood. What does that mean?" he practically shouted into the phone.

"Sir, calm down. An ambulance is on the way. Is she breathing?"

Evan caught the shallow rise and fall of Natalie's chest. "Yes, but she doesn't look good. Hurry!"

The sound of the ambulance wailing cut into the operator's next sentence and Evan said a hurried thank-you before disconnecting. His heart was hammering and sweat covered his body as he stared at Natalie, anguish and guilt colliding into one another as he glanced at the ladder and immediately surmised what had happened. The dragon, fierce and commanding, stared down at them in an impressive show of dominance, wings spread and nostrils flaring and he knew. She'd been on the ladder finishing her masterpiece. He swore, blaming himself for not being there. Flushing from the emotion crowding his heart, he moved aside for the paramedics and watched as they did their jobs.

The paramedic from the first time Natalie had fainted in her apartment assessed her vitals, a frown creasing his young face. He turned to Evan.

"How far along is she?"

"Six and a half months."

Natalie stirred, moaning as her eyelids fluttered. Her hands immediately flew to her stomach and Evan fought the urge to follow suit.

"The baby," she moaned, her voice weak and raspy.

"Ma'am, try not to move. We're going to take you to the hospital right now. Sir, do you want to ride with her?"

The young man barely gave Evan time to decide before he pushed past him to load Natalie into the ambulance. Going on instinct, he jumped in beside her and immediately grasped her hand. It felt cold to the touch and fear struck his heart. What if she died? There was a lot of blood on the floor and he had no idea how long she'd lain there. Damn it! Why didn't anyone see she was lying on the floor? Where was that nosey sister of hers when she needed her? What the hell had he been thinking? Traipsing off to the ranch knowing full well she'd think nothing of climbing that damn ladder without anyone around. Foolish on both their parts!

The ambulance screamed around the corner, barreling past the slow-moving traffic that made up half the population in the small town, and pulled into the emergency bay. The doors flew open and Evan barely had time to get out of the way before Natalie was wheeled out and into the E.R. His only choice was to follow or get the hell out of the way.

And one thing was for sure—this time around he wasn't going to leave her alone.

CHAPTER NINETEEN

NATALIE OPENED her eyes and tried to focus. Recognition came slowly as odd sound blips assaulted her ears and the sterile white room of a hospital came into view. Her mouth felt filled with cotton and her head weighted down with cement. She turned and saw Evan sprawled in the small courtesy chair beside the window, his legs spread out before him like stilts and his head settled on the cushion at an uncomfortable angle.

"Evan?" she managed to croak, her voice awakening him. He straightened, scrubbing his hands across his face, and stiffly pulled himself out of the chair to stand beside her. His expression was a cross between tender and concerned and tears filled her eyes as she voiced her worst fear. "The baby?"

Evan started to answer but the doctor

entered first and Natalie's heart stopped when she read his stern expression.

"Oh, God," she whispered, shaking her head, not wanting to hear what he had to say. *Please*...

"Your baby," the doctor said, coming to her bedside, "is going to be fine, provided you stop falling from ladders. In fact, let's avoid ladders all together, shall we?"

Relief made her shoulders sag as a different set of tears broke loose and cascaded down her cheeks. Unable to stop them, she buried her face in her palms and simply bawled. She felt Evan lightly rub her shoulders, and she took comfort in the small gesture. She wanted to curl into his arms and sob against the solid wall of his chest but she didn't have the right. She'd almost killed their child with her stubborn determination to finish that stupid mural when she knew she'd been too tired to be on that ladder safely. Lifting her head she accepted a tissue from the doctor, who had waited patiently for her outburst to end before continuing.

"What happened?" she asked once she had a voice to speak with. "I mean, when I fell?"

"You had an abruption," he explained, his

gaze moving from Natalie to Evan. "Luckily for you and your baby, it was relatively minor."

"Minor?" Evan repeated incredulously. "There was an awful lot of blood there, doc. Are you sure everything's all right in there?"

"Yes, we did a preliminary ultrasound when she was brought into the E.R. but we're going to check again to be sure. That's what I was coming in to tell you."

"An ultrasound?" Evan's voice cracked a little. "You mean, right now? Will we be able to see the baby?"

The doctor nodded. "Yes. We'll be using the 3-D ultrasound machine, state-of-the-art." He turned toward the door. "I think I hear the nurse rolling it down the hall as we speak. Are you ready to see your son or daughter?"

EVAN SWALLOWED but his mouth was drier than the Sahara. He shot a look to Natalie, who looked just as shocked, and watched as the nurse entered with a large contraption that looked like something out of a futuristic movie.

The nurse smiled warmly as she slid the machine into place. "I heard you had a little bit of a scare today," she said to Natalie in a conversational tone as she readied the machine, which had begun to whir softly as it warmed up. "Let's see what's going on," she said, lifting Natalie's gown to smear a jelly substance across her belly. After a quick adjustment to the controls, a picture appeared though nothing was showing just yet. Then the nurse placed a bulbous, funny-looking wand against the smooth, slicked-up skin of Natalie's stomach.

At first Evan couldn't see anything more distinguishable than a bunch of flecks that looked as if she'd trained headlights into a snow flurry, but after a flick of her wrist using the roller ball on the console, the sound of a rapidly beating heart filled the room and Evan could see his baby floating in the safety of a fluid-filled cocoon.

The breath escaped his body in a painful whoosh and he couldn't swallow properly. Unexpected tears filled his eyes and he had to blink them back furiously before he embarrassed himself in front of Natalie and a complete stranger. "Is he—or she—okay?"

"Looks good so far. Strong heartbeat this one. No worries at least in that department," the doctor said, taking over for the nurse so he could get a better look.

A perfectly shaped, tiny hand came into view and Evan leaned in closer, his chest wall close to Natalie's head. Anyone happening to catch a glimpse of the scene might naturally assume they'd seen a happy couple getting misty-eyed over their first child, and for a wild, disconcerting moment he wished with all his heart those were truly the circumstances between them. He wanted the freedom to hold Natalie's hand tight in his own as they faced down the fear or embraced the miracle. But as it was, the closest he could get to Natalie was the brief touch they shared as he crowded near to get a better look at his child. Their child. This time the tears that appeared had nothing to do with the miracle of life. For the first time since Hailey he wanted *more*.

"Can you tell what the sex of the baby is yet?" Natalie asked, shooting a tentative look at Evan as if asking if he wanted to know as well. He reassured her with a nod and they both looked to the doctor.

"With this machine I can see the baby's facial expression," the doctor joked, moving the wand into a more favorable position. "Do you want to know?"

"Yes," they said in unison.

"I thought so." He made some more adjustments and then pointed to the screen. "There you go. The package."

"By the 'package' do you mean…" Excitement warred with joy as Evan arched his brow at the doctor, but Natalie looked confused and stared harder at the screen. The doctor nodded, and Evan's smile broadened. "Natalie," he said, his voice choked, "we're having a son."

"A son?" she whispered, her bottom lip trembling and her eyes watering. "A son," she repeated to herself as if in wonder or shock or a little of both. She sent him a tremulous smile and Evan didn't think twice before bending down and placing a tender kiss on her lips. He pulled away and looked deep into her eyes, wishing he could name all the emotions bursting in his heart and going every which direction. But, honestly, he wasn't sure his mouth would've cooperated.

The doctor cleared his throat and Evan remembered they weren't alone. Reluctant to sever the moment, he pulled away slowly. Regret intruded on his elation but he hid it well, not wanting to ruin the moment for Natalie.

The doctor moved the wand toward the cervical opening and the baby was replaced by a view of the uterus. Evan couldn't help but feel disappointed until the doctor spoke again, his voice grave. "Well, this is our problem here." He pointed to a small dark bubble on the screen. "That right there is a blood clot from your abruption earlier this evening."

"What does that mean?" Natalie asked, her voice fearful.

"It means, you're on bed rest for a week or two to make sure this doesn't turn into a bigger complication."

"Bed rest?" she echoed, her gaze flitting to Evan as if he could explain what that meant exactly.

"What do you mean by bed rest?" Evan asked for her.

The doctor chuckled. "It means total bed rest with only bathroom privileges. No climbing ladders, no painting ceilings, no water-skiing, no getting up to get yourself a bowl of cereal." He gestured to Evan with a good-natured smile. "Let your husband make himself useful. Now's the time to cash in all those honey-do requests. Enjoy being pampered for a while. Because—" the jocularity fled from his voice as his eyes focused alternately between the two of them "—your baby's life may depend on it. That spot where the abruption occurred is extremely vulnerable. If you were to go into labor right now, the odds of your baby's survival are slim. And as you've already seen, an abruption can cause rapid blood loss. If you have another abruption on this scale or larger…we might lose you, too."

Evan looked to Natalie and he had no doubt her ashen face was surely a reflection of his own, but the doctor smiled and patted Evan on the shoulder as if he hadn't just delivered a shocking statement and gave the nurse the go-ahead to pack up.

"Cheer up, son. These things are rare, but they are serious. Help this little lady take it easy for a few weeks and we'll reevaluate her condition. Until then—" he wagged a finger at Natalie "—off your feet."

Off her feet? *Impossible*…Natalie started to protest but the doctor was already leaving, heading to his next patient. What about her bookstore? How would she open in time if she spent the day flat on her back? And what about Evan? She couldn't expect him to be her beck-and-call boy, no matter how much the idea played too well into her fantasies. She dropped her head into her hands and her shoulders shook with the silent tears she was trying desperately to squeeze back.

"Natalie?" Evan gently pulled her hands down and peered into her face. "It's going to be all right. Don't worry."

"How, Evan? How is it going to be all right?" The fear roiling her belly gave an edge to her voice. "I've put *everything* I own into that store. How am I going to finish in time if I'm stuck on bed rest?"

"Well, like the doctor said…put me to use." He grinned broadly and Natalie wanted to groan into her pillow. "What?" he asked, frowning when she didn't seem to see the humor.

"You're not my husband and it doesn't do either of us any good to pretend otherwise," she said quietly, ignoring the ache in her chest. "My problems are not your problems. We have other issues to deal with. Let's not complicate it any further."

"Too late," he said simply before descending to her level until he was inches from her face. Her heart rate picked up speed and her breath became shallow as she yearned to just close the distance and feel his lips again. Their kiss moments ago had been excruciatingly short, teasing her with its promise for more, and her dreams were becoming a poor substitute for what she really wanted. "We're in this together," he said, his warm breath tickling her face. "And I'm not leaving, so get used to it."

"But," she started, until Evan sealed his lips to hers, swallowing her weak protest as he slanted his mouth, taking and tasting in a way that left no room for denial on her part. In truth, she could've drowned in the dizzying tumult of sensation spiraling through her body with little resistance. She could spend a lifetime in exactly this same position, she realized dreamily.

"What the hell is going on here?"

Natalie gasped and instinctively pushed Evan away as the sound of her father's outraged voice registered with crystal clarity. She tried a tremulous smile but it faded in the face of her father's scowl and her mother's knitted brows as she trailed behind him. "Daddy—" she said hesitantly, but Gerald's attention was focused on Evan.

"Who are you and what do you think you're doing pawing my daughter? Don't they have security around here?"

Most people quailed when Gerald Simmons growled, much less bellowed, but Evan didn't falter. "If you're the coward who knocked up my daughter, you can just keep your hands off. You've done enough damage to this family," he sputtered, sending a venomous look Evan's way.

"Daddy," Natalie implored, pleading with her mother to intervene, or at least try to defuse the situation before things got out of hand. "Lower your voice, you're in a hospital."

Evan watched the scene with narrowed vision but when he glanced at Natalie, his expression softened as if to say he was willing to make the effort for her benefit. He cleared his throat. "Yes, sir, I am that guy but I'm not *that guy* you seem to have in your head. I aim to be a father to my child if that's what you're worried about. Name's Evan Murphy. Pleased to meet you."

The glower on her father's face didn't bode well for anyone. Evan came forward with his hand outstretched, though Natalie knew he had a snowball's chance in hell of receiving a reciprocal gesture from her father. Still, it warmed her in silly romantic places that he would try.

"You going to marry her?" Gerald said, ignoring Evan's hand until he withdrew it to cross his arms against his chest, meeting her father's hard stare.

Natalie cringed, sensing Evan was the last person who'd consider marriage under these circumstances. She tried to intervene but she was shushed like a child.

"Daddy!" she said, her temper flaring from an unexpected place. She never yelled, much less raised her voice to her father, but he was getting out of hand. "I'm thirty-two years old. I don't need you forcing Evan to the altar. We'll figure this thing out on our own. Besides—" she drew a deep steadying breath now that she had everyone's attention "—I wouldn't marry him if he asked."

This time it was Evan's turn to look startled. He turned to her, his brow wrinkling in confusion. "You wouldn't?" he asked, his voice reflecting a hurt ego, but Natalie couldn't back down, especially with her father standing there, judging them both.

"I don't really want to get in to this right

now." Smoothing her hand over her belly, she drew strength from the fact that her son was safe despite her ordeal. "What's most important is the health of my baby," she said, a small smile forming as she looked to her parents. Her voice broke as she added meaningfully, "Your grandson."

"Grandson?" Gerald's face lit up, but not before sending Evan a hard look. "How do you know already?"

Missy came forward, a gentle smile on her face. "We came as soon as we heard. Is everything...all right? The admitting nurse said you took a tumble off a ladder."

"I'm fine," she answered, clarifying quickly when Evan frowned. "Uh, well, I've been put on bed rest for a few weeks. It seems I had an abruption when I fell. So, the doctor doesn't want to chance another and has prescribed complete bed rest for a little while."

Evan shifted on the balls of his feet and Natalie sensed his discomfort. The previous intimacy of the moment faded into a distant memory, if not a total fabrication of her imagination, and she wasn't surprised when he excused himself. There was no kiss goodbye, nothing of the sweetness she'd tasted only moments ago before her father came in and ruined everything, but she couldn't say she blamed Evan for not feeling very romantic. She bit back a disappointed sigh but was unable to keep her gaze from tracking him as he left the room with a loose promise to call later.

"He is the father, isn't he?" Missy ventured, sending a nervous look to Gerald before returning to Natalie.

"Yes," she admitted, liking the way the affirmation sounded on her tongue. "He is."

"Why's he coming around now? Where was he when you were on that ladder?"

"That's not fair," she admonished. "He had no idea I was going to finish the mural. In fact, if anyone's to blame, I am." She lowered her gaze. "I knew I was too tired to be on the ladder safely but I wanted to finish what I'd started. I was being stubborn."

Her father nodded but she could tell he was still troubled. "I don't like him," he announced. "He's an arrogant son of a bitch."

"Gerald," Missy said in a softly warning tone. "It's none of our business."

"She's our daughter—that makes it our business," he retorted. "He went and got her pregnant and then just deserted her. As far as I'm concerned he's not welcome in this family."

"Dad—" She wanted to defend Evan, needed to, but her father held up his hand, signaling he was finished with the conversation. Natalie pressed her lips together in frustration, knowing her father's mind was made up and it would take a stick of dynamite to change it. It shouldn't matter. She and Evan had no real future. But it did. It mattered a lot. Tears crowded her sinuses and she turned away as he left the room. For the first time, she understood Nora's aggravation toward their father. She'd always known it was "his way or the highway," only it had never adversely affected her in the past.

Now it wasn't so simple. But she wasn't prepared to lose her father for a man who had no discernable path in life aside from the meandering one that took him from one destination to another. She wanted more.

Too bad Evan was the last person equipped to offer.

CHAPTER TWENTY

EVAN APPEARED in the doorway of her hospital room just as she was grabbing her bags to leave. She'd spent the night, but Nora was on her way to pick her up and take her home. When he saw her standing, his expression darkened.

"Total bed rest," he reminded her, pointing toward the bed as he strode forward. "It's a good thing I showed up when I did. What are you doing?"

She scowled, unaccustomed to having someone watch her every move. "I do have bathroom privileges, you know."

His gaze dropped quizzically to the bag in her hand. "And that's where you were going?"

"Well, no, I was getting ready to leave. Nora should be here any minute."

"Why didn't you call me?"

She blushed as he awaited her answer.

"Evan...I know we have some things to work out but we shouldn't complicate—"

"It's not complicated," he said, disagreeing even as he relieved her of the small bag in her hand. "You've been ordered on bed rest. I live right below you. The simple answer is for you to move in with me."

Move in? Spots threatened to dance before her eyes at the very thought. It was bad enough having him directly beneath her but to be in the same small apartment? No way. No how. Not. In. A. Million. Years. "You've lost your mind," she said, reaching for her bag. He lifted it away, out of reach. "What are you doing?" she asked, exasperation coloring her voice.

"Trying to talk some sense into your hard head." He shouldered her bag. A man shouldn't look so hot without even trying, she thought grumpily. She remembered in precise detail how those broad shoulders felt under her fingertips. Thanks to her dreams, if you could call them that—they seemed more like fodder for the Spice channel—she was bombarded with a sensory overload of possibilities that they hadn't had time to tap during their short dalliance. He crooked a grin at her as if he'd just caught a glimpse of what had just been running through her head, eliciting a frown on her part. "What are you afraid of? Think I'll try to seduce you?"

Immediately stung by how ridiculous that statement sounded, despite the fact that he was the one who'd helped put her in this situation, she shot him a nasty look. "I'm afraid of no such thing. I know I'm hardly fantasy material at present…thanks to you," she couldn't help but add. The sound of his laughter startled her. Insecurity made her voice sound petulant. "What's so funny?"

"You," he stated simply, sending her another smile that threatened to melt her defenses quicker than paraffin candle wax against an open flame. He sobered and pointed at the bed. "Take a seat. I'll be right back with a wheelchair."

"I'm not sure that's necessary," she called after him just as Nora appeared in the doorway, doing a double take.

"Was that Evan?" When Natalie nodded, she gave her a quizzical look. "What's he doing here? I thought I was picking you up."

"He just showed up. I didn't know he was going to do that."

"How sweet of him," Nora cooed until

Natalie sent her an evil look. "You're such a sourpuss these days. It's a miracle anyone wants to spend any time with you."

"He wants me to move in with him," she said, ignoring Nora's last comment. "What should I do?"

"Do you want to move in with him?" Nora's blunt question made her blush and her sister laughed. "So, what's holding you back? You're already pregnant…what else could happen?"

Natalie bit back a groan and sent her sister another dark look. "Plenty," she growled, glad Nora wasn't aware of the R-rated scenarios flipping through her brain at the thought of moving in with Evan. She cleared her throat and willed her blood to cool. "Besides, the last thing we need to do is complicate things."

Nora rolled her eyes and gestured for her to get up. "Fine, Nat. Do it your way. The boring way, I might add, and ensure that nothing gets messy or *complicated* as you put it. Sometimes I wonder that we share the same genes."

"You and me both," Natalie grumbled, taking offense at Nora's comment. She shelved her retort in favor of leaving before Evan returned with that wheelchair.

But it was too late. Evan appeared just as they were rounding the corner.

"Whoa there," Evan exclaimed when they nearly collided with one another.

"Long time no see," Nora quipped, grinning despite the despairing look Natalie sent her. She glanced down at the chair. "Nice ride."

"Thanks. Too bad your sister doesn't agree," he returned pointedly, his tone making Natalie feel like an errant child for obviously trying to skip out on his offer. No, it wasn't really an offer, she clarified, lifting her chin. It was a dictate.

He pointed at the seat. "It's either in the chair or in my arms but either way you're not walking out of this hospital."

"How romantic," Nora giggled, barely able to hide the laughter from her voice. Not even a sour look from Natalie could remove the silly grin from her face. "Well, it is," she said, defending herself when Natalie didn't share the sentiment.

"If you think it's so romantic why don't you take a ride on the Evan Express. I, for one, don't feel it's necessary to ride out of the hospital in a wheelchair. I'm not an invalid."

"No, you're on bed rest, or have you forgotten what put you there in the first place?"

"I..." Natalie shifted under the suddenly serious stares of both Evan and her sister. She could hardly argue with Evan's point. The fight went out of her and her hand went to the rounded area of her belly. "Fine," she conceded, moving gingerly into the chair with an unhappy sigh. "But we're not sleeping in the same bed. If I'm going to stay at your apartment, you're taking the couch!"

Evan's amused chuckle coupled with Nora's surprised laughter from behind curved her lips into a reluctant smile as Evan wheeled her out of the hospital. Nora wasn't the only Simmons woman who was capable of wild and crazy things.

IT WAS A BOLD MOVE; one he was sure Natalie would vehemently disagree with, but seeing his child move on the ultrasound screen had sharpened his focus in a way nothing ever had. If his child's life depended on Natalie remaining on bed rest, he'd make sure that's exactly what happened. And the only way he could ensure she didn't move from a reclining position was to keep her with him at all times. He could say he was being practical but he knew it went deeper. It was useless to lie, even to himself. He wanted Natalie with him. The sight of her growing stomach filled him with a sense of pride that was primal and he yearned to wrap his arms around her, to draw her and their baby cocooned in her belly close.

"I mean it about the bed," Natalie said, breaking into his thoughts as he settled her on the sofa, tucking a soft throw blanket around her feet when she complained of cold toes. Her eyes followed him, the uncertainty in them making him want to kiss her breathless if only to chase away the insecurity he saw there. She'd thought he didn't think she was sexy due to her growing size, but it was just the opposite. The only thing holding him in check was the doctor's strict instructions, *no nooky*. She looked away, misreading his subtle frown, her cheeks flushing prettily. "Forget I said anything," she whispered.

"Listen," he said, kneeling before her, enjoying the way her eyes widened as he slid his hand across her belly in a way that was tender yet possessive. "We've got a lot to figure out but I know if it weren't for the doctor's orders, there's not a lot that would stand in my way from making love to you."

"Evan…" His name came out in an adorable squeak as her forehead wrinkled at his admission and for a brief, painful moment he wondered if he'd just bared his soul to someone who didn't share the same feelings, but when tears filled her eyes he knew that wasn't the problem. Elation crowded his breast until she dropped her head into her hands and started to bawl.

"What's wrong?" Alarm colored his voice as he gently drew her hands away from her face. "You can tell me anything, Natalie. I promise I'll try to make whatever's bothering you better."

His offer only made her sob harder. Tension corded his shoulders as confusion collided with frustration when she wouldn't stop to answer his queries. Finally, she hiccuped and stopped long enough to say, "Oh, Evan, why are we doing this? I don't want you to be like this."

"Like what?"

She gestured wildly. "Like *this!* Warm, caring and sweet."

He drew back. "That's an odd complaint. Why not?"

She looked miserable. "Because that's how you were in Utah and if you act like that here, now with me all big and pregnant, these stupid hormones will make me feel things that aren't real."

He searched for the right words, but he was at a complete loss. She wasn't making much sense. He scratched his head. "What's not real? We're having a baby together. That's as real as it gets in my book."

Her throat bobbed in another watery hiccup, her eyes sad. "You and me…we're not real. Whatever we're feeling isn't genuine. Your feelings for me are twisted into your feelings for the baby." He started to balk but she continued in earnest, wiping her nose with the back of her hand as she did. "Can you honestly say that you'd have stayed if I wasn't pregnant? C'mon, Evan… you're a confirmed bachelor with no reason before now to put down roots—aside from a bedroom at the ranch you barely use. And right now, with all the hormones rushing through my body, I can't be sure that what I'm feeling isn't a by-product of the baby needing extra progesterone or whatever hormone makes you feel like you're hot and cold all at once so you don't know whether you need to shiver or tear your clothes off."

"Is that how I make you feel?" he asked softly.

"What?"

He came closer. "I said, is that how I make you feel. Hot and cold. All at once?"

She bit her lip, drawing his gaze to the fleshy, pink skin. "Yes," she admitted in a whisper, watching warily as he came closer. "But that's not good," she protested with a frown.

"Sounds terrible," he agreed, focused on the inviting flesh caught between her teeth. "But let's test your theory," he said, moving in for a taste. She gasped into his mouth, providing the perfect opportunity to slide his tongue in, as his hand continued to gently palm her belly. She softened under his touch and it took everything in him not to pull her pants down and press a hot trail to the place her panties hid from view but not from his memory. Chest moving with the breath made shallow by his accelerated heart rate, he reluctantly pulled away, breaking contact. He was inordinately pleased to see she was suffering under the same effect. Removing his hand, he raked it through his hair and offered a grin. "I think you may be right about one thing," he said, his gaze roaming over her body as his own tightened with pent-up desire.

"Which is…?" came her breathless response.

"This might be a bad idea." He broke out into a teasing grin, adding with a negligent shrug, "But then again, that didn't stop us the last time, did it?"

CHAPTER TWENTY-ONE

"Upsy daisy!" Evan lifted Natalie and cradled her to his chest.

"Evan, this isn't necessary. I feel ridiculous," Natalie grumbled, yet her arms wound around his neck as he carried her to his truck. "The doctor didn't say you needed to carry me everywhere."

"Well, look at it this way, in a few more months I probably won't be able to lift you anyway, so enjoy it while you can."

She gasped in outrage at his comment and a deep-throated chuckle rumbled from his chest. "Don't you know you're never supposed to point out to a pregnant woman how big she's getting? It's rude." She sniffed, lifting her nose in the air in a way that made him want to kiss the tip.

"I'll remember that for the next time I knock someone up." He caught a glare from his peripheral vision and a sudden burn in his ear followed. "Ow! Did you just flick me?" he asked, incredulous.

"You deserved it."

Okay, he probably did, he thought as he silently chuckled, but his spirits soared. She didn't like the idea of him being with someone else. In his book that showed promise. For what, he wasn't sure, but he was game to find out.

Arriving at the bookstore, Evan unloaded a folding chaise lounge and a few pillows for Natalie before retrieving her from the truck. She was still grumbling about the inconvenience and the embarrassment but it didn't deter him. The way he saw it, this was a good compromise. The doctor wanted her resting and Natalie wanted to be at the shop…well, there you go, he thought as he finished putting Natalie's little resting area together.

"How am I supposed to just lie here while you do all the work?" she asked, her gaze following him as he rearranged boxes so there was a clear path. When he didn't answer right away a groan of frustration escaped until she pressed her lips together tightly, her expression sullen.

"Hold that thought," he said as he walked

out the door. He returned from the truck and tossed a magazine to her, which she caught easily. "Here, some reading material in case you get bored."

In spite of her obvious annoyance, she smiled when she read the cover. "*Us Magazine*? Interesting choice." Tilting her head at him, she arched her brow, asking, "What made you choose this?"

"This is great stuff. Who doesn't care about who's sleeping with who in Hollywood?" he insisted with mock seriousness. "Besides, isn't this what all women like to read while they're waiting in line at the grocery store? Don't lie, I've seen them do it."

A genuine smile lit her face as she conceded. "Okay, you got me there. It's a guilty pleasure."

"Well, feel free to enjoy your Hollywood gossip in relative anonymity." He rubbed his hands together, anxious to start working. Eyeing the boxes he'd just muscled out of the way, he pointed. "Let's start with these."

He dragged the boxes over to Natalie and, after he carefully slit the top open with a razor, she opened each one and exclaimed at the contents. "Ohhh, look at all these fabulous books!" She hefted a thick book, angling it toward Evan and crowed. "It's the new Harry Potter!" Before Evan had time to comment, she'd grabbed another. "Lemony Snicket! Fantastic!"

Lemony what? "What the hell is a Lemony Snicket?"

"It's a *very* popular children's series, the first three were made into a movie. But, they're a bit hard to explain if you aren't a fan," she admitted with a shrug. It was as if offering him an explanation was a waste of everyone's time as he was the last person who'd ever pick up a Snicket book. Evan stiffened at the assumption and tucked a copy under his arm. "Where are you going with that?" she asked, frowning.

"Consider me your first customer. I'm going to read what this—" he grabbed the book and gave it a quick perusal "—series of unfortunate events is all about. I love a good book."

Her mouth curved in a reluctant, yet warm smile and he smiled back. "Where do you want these literary masterpieces?" he asked.

"The middle shelf, thank you."

He began unloading the boxes, placing the

books in a neat and tidy line on the shelves while Natalie catalogued the inventory into a small laptop that looked as if it had seen better days and they each settled into a quiet routine. The sun began sinking low in the horizon and Evan looked over at Natalie to find her dozing, her hand resting on the bump that was their child. A sense of protectiveness washed over him and he exhaled lightly, as the reality of their situation stared back at him. He had feelings for this woman. Unease prickled the back of his neck at the vulnerability his admission caused. Did they have a future? Was Natalie right? Was he confusing his feelings toward the baby with feelings toward her? He wasn't sure but he couldn't deny that he wanted to be around her all the time, wanted to be a partner in the raising of their child. Yet, soon he'd have to leave to replenish the cash he was spending. As soon as the first snow fell, he was already scheduled to show up at Dodge Ridge, the ski lodge near Pinecrest, for his gig as a ski instructor but the idea of leaving Natalie wasn't appealing. *Neither is not being able to afford diapers,* a voice reminded him. He sighed—time was running out and he had to figure out something.

NATALIE FIDGETED with the end of the blanket Evan had draped across her legs and craned her neck to try and catch a glimpse of him in the kitchen. "Are you sure I can't help you do something?" she asked, her stomach growling at the savory smells emanating from that general area.

"Everything's about ready. Just sit tight."

That's all she'd been doing for a week, she wanted to retort, settling back against the sofa cushion. "Easy for you to say…you're not the one who's forbidden to get up and get a drink of water for yourself."

Evan popped his head around the corner, concern etched on his face. "Are you thirsty?"

She rolled her eyes but a giggle tickled her chest. "*No*, I'm just using that as an example. So, what are you making? I should tell you I'm allergic to mushrooms."

"What happens when you eat one?" His voice carried over the sounds in the kitchen. "Do you puff up and get all itchy or keel over in anaphylactic shock?"

"Uh, well, seeing as I'm not dead, I'd say the first one. I get hives all over and I look like a puffer fish. Not very attractive."

A chuckle followed and Natalie smiled in

the safety of the living room. "No mushrooms. Scout's honor."

"Like you were ever a Boy Scout," she wisecracked, prompting an indignant exclamation from the other side. Evan appeared carrying a plate laden with pork chops, green salad and a slice of French bread heavy on the butter and garlic. Her mouth salivated as she accepted the plate eagerly. "Ohh, where'd you learn to cook like this?"

He shrugged, taking his place beside her. "Here and there, but mostly Jonesy. He took pity on the poor college kid who couldn't do much more than boil water when we first met."

"Where'd you go to college?" she asked in between bites. When he hesitated, she said, "Let me guess…here and there."

He swallowed as he grinned. "You got it."

The food was amazing but Evan's obvious reluctance to share anything personal kept her from completely enjoying it. She slid a sideways glance at him, taking in his lean physique and her breath quickened. The effect he had on her was devastating to her sense of logic. When she was around him, she wanted to curl herself into his lap like a contented kitten until reality intruded and she realized no amount of contortions were going to curl her body into any semblance of something as agile as a cat and her mood plummeted. Evan, as if sensing her quiet assessment, turned, catching her off guard.

"Like what you see?"

His tone was playful but the expression in his dark eyes was nothing but sultry and she found herself nodding until she realized what she was doing and returned to her plate with heated cheeks. "Sorry," she said, taking a hasty bite of pork chop.

They ate in silence until Natalie thought she might die from the questions giving her mind no amount of peace. She needed answers. As much as she privately enjoyed playing house, they were running out of time.

"Evan?" She placed her nearly empty plate on the floor and took a deep breath. When she had his attention, she plunged forward. "I need to know what your intentions are."

He made a choking sound and reached for his water glass. "Excuse me?" he said, once his trachea was clear of the food he'd been chewing. "Intentions? That sounds so Victorian. What do you mean?"

She twisted her hands in the blanket. "You

know…about the baby. He's going to be here before we know it. I don't even know where you live!"

He sobered from the serious note in her voice and looked almost guilty. A long pause followed as he struggled with an answer and she fought against a general sense of unease. "Is it a secret or something?" she asked, half-serious. "Why don't you like to talk about anything personal?"

He shrugged but avoided eye contact. "It's just not very interesting."

"It's interesting to me," she insisted, trying to catch his eye. When he finally glanced up, she tried using a smile to disarm him. "It can't be that bad."

"Who said it was bad?" he countered sharply and she drew back. He shook his head in apology. "I didn't mean to snap. I'm just not the kind of person to dwell on the past. That's why I don't bring it up much."

"Fair enough," she said, yet she was troubled. What could be so bad that he didn't want to talk about it? She tried changing direction. "Let's talk about our plans for when the baby arrives."

"We've got some time still," he said with a forced smile that only intensified her growing concern. "Besides, we need to focus on keeping junior in the oven, and all that involves is me seeing to your every need. Sound good?"

He came to pick up her plate and she accepted the peck he placed on the top of her head. She yearned to just go with the flow but that just wasn't in her nature. She needed answers or she'd worry and fret until it ruined whatever peace they had between them. An unhappy sigh escaped and the baby kicked, reminding her of his precarious position and reinforcing the decision she needed to make.

She cleared her voice in the hopes that when she spoke it sounded steady and strong, but despite her efforts, there was a slight tremble. "Evan, I appreciate everything you've done for me and the baby but...I don't think I can stay here anymore."

"What?" he asked, coming from the kitchen, his expression forming a dark scowl. "Where's this coming from?"

"I—I'm becoming confused and the last time I was confused it put me in this position.

I need to be smart and being here with you…is the opposite of smart right now."

"You need someone to take care of you while you're on bed rest," he countered tersely. "Let's keep the big picture in view here."

"It's more than that and you know it," she asserted firmly. "We have chemistry and it makes it hard to know which end is up sometimes. Playing house isn't helping matters." She drew a deep breath and when she continued she couldn't help the resignation in her tone. "We're not a couple. We're…I don't know what we are."

"We're going to be parents. That should count for something."

"It does," she agreed in earnest. "And yet, you don't want to share a single private detail about yourself. What does that tell you?"

A muscle in his jaw jumped as the silence lengthened.

"Evan…"

"You're right," he said stonily and her heart plummeted. He could've tried harder to change her mind. All he had to do was open himself up to her. Why was that so difficult? His gaze dropped to the floor and she wondered if he saw the pieces of her heart on the shaggy carpet. "I don't seem to have the answers you need. All I can say is I'm doing the best that I can."

She believed him but it wasn't good enough with a baby on the way. She wiped at her nose and said, "I'll make arrangements with Nora. I'm sure she'll help me out if I ask."

He nodded but his expression had dimmed.

"I'm not trying to hurt your feelings—" She stopped when he turned abruptly and returned to the kitchen. She sensed his withdrawal and almost wished she hadn't said anything, but ignoring the truth didn't make it go away. "I just want—"

"What's best." He reappeared, finishing her sentence with a subtle sneer. "I know. That's all I ever hear from you." Her eyes widened as his temper flared. He tossed the hand towel he'd wiped his hands with to the counter. "Natalie, did you ever stop to consider that maybe what's best isn't what you've got stuck in your head? Who says your way is the best way?"

Stung, she tried defending herself but he was too angry to listen.

"You're right. I don't have a clue as to what

I'm going to do when the baby gets here. All I know is I'll love him with everything I have because I already do. And you're right—I don't know if my feelings for you are tangled up with feelings for the baby but they're there just the same. What do we do? I don't know. But, I'm willing to try and find out if you are."

Her heart sped up at the possibility, wanting so much to do exactly as he suggested, but she knew that path was filled with heartbreak. "Evan, you don't even have a regular job! How are you supposed to support this baby?"

He raked a hand through his hair. "I don't know yet, but I'm working on it!"

Sadness enveloped her and she shook her head. "That's not good enough. I need more than just a vague game plan. We aren't living in a fairy tale. It's not possible to live on love!"

He looked at her sharply and she realized she'd made a Freudian slip with regard to her own feelings. "I mean, it's…not that we're in love, I'm not saying," she stammered, her cheeks heating furiously until she was surely red enough to light the neighborhood. "All I'm saying is…oh, forget it! You obviously don't understand what I'm trying to say."

The anger tightening his face sharpened his features and he surprised her with a short jerk of his head as he brusquely agreed. "You're right. You need more. I'm sorry." He grabbed his keys, placed the portable phone beside her, then went to the door. "I'll be back. I need some fresh air."

The door closed behind him and Natalie was half-tempted to throw off the blankets and chase after him. What good would that do? Aside from make her look like a clinging ninny. The baby kicked again and Natalie slid her palm across the width in a reassuring motion, but she felt anything but reassured at the moment. Was Evan right? Maybe she was only willing to see things from her point of view but, damn it, it didn't seem very smart to go about something this important without a game plan. She just wanted what was best for her baby. *So, stop trying to exclude the father,* a voice shot back in the privacy of her mind. *I'm not trying to,* she wanted to wail in frustration, but a small part of her realized she might be doing just that to protect herself. Oh great. She could spend all night arguing with herself like a complete crazy person or she could do something proactive. Like what? She was stuck on the couch. Scratch that. At least she could wait for Evan to return and apologize. Drawing a deep breath, Natalie calmed herself with a plan.

EVAN GUNNED THE TRUCK, bouncing down the country dirt road, not caring where he ended up. He just needed to drive. It helped to clear his head when it felt filled with straw. And right now he was about as straw-filled as a scarecrow. If he wasn't in such a foul mood, he would've laughed at his poorly constructed simile. And to think, he was the one with the advanced education.

The road curved without warning and his tires skidded against the dirt, seeking traction. Heart racing, suddenly he was grateful for his decision to pay a little extra for new tires. Straightening, he eased up on the gas and berated himself for driving like an idiot. A wide shoulder appeared out of the darkness and he pulled off the road.

He couldn't blame Natalie for wanting more. He wanted more, too. But what did he have to offer? Pride burned a hole into his gut as he shook his head at the irony. With Hailey, he'd been ready and perfectly able to give her the world. His future looked bright. Headhunters for top corporations had earmarked his resume and from the looks of it, he was going to write his ticket to big-time money if he played his cards right. Yeah, he'd been a little cocky, he acknowledged, thinking back on those days, but he'd earned it after finishing at the top of his class at graduate school. Hailey, bright, beautiful and aggressive; he'd thought they were the perfect pair. What an illusion.

Sighing, he leaned against his headrest and wondered how to clean up the mess he'd made with Natalie. But first, he had to find a job.

Time to tap some old friendships.

CHAPTER TWENTY-TWO

NATALIE DIDN'T HEAR Evan return. Despite her intention to stay awake, she was dead to the world within an hour of her decision. She awoke the next morning tucked into Evan's bed.

Stretching languidly, she inhaled Evan's subtle scent that clung to his sheets and smiled dreamily, not quite awake. He had the most wonderfully delightful smell, she thought. A woman could get used to this.

The familiar screech of a truck door opening and slamming shut intruded and she jerked awake. Nora?

Flinging the covers to the side, she ignored the doctor's orders and walked slowly into the living room just in time to see Nora open the door.

"Morning sunshine," she said brightly, ignoring Natalie's obvious bed-head and state of dress, or lack thereof, she realized in embarrassment. She tugged at her tank top but her belly poked out just the same. "Nice duds," she remarked casually but added with a raised brow, "but if you're still trying to seduce the guy you might look into something that doesn't include granny panties."

"I'm not trying to seduce him," she shot back before disappearing to put on a pair of shorts. "Besides, right now, it's all about comfort," she said defensively, yet privately grimaced as she pictured Evan's reaction when he undressed her for bed last night. *Way to knock him off his feet, Nat.*

"What are you doing here?" she asked, rounding the corner again, heading for the kitchen.

"Helping you. Evan stopped by my place and said you'd need my help since he was going to be gone for about a week. I'm here to pick you up."

Oh. Natalie's spirits plummeted. Of all the times to take her seriously! He could've tried just a teensy bit harder to change her mind. "Did he say where he was going?" she asked.

"Nope. Why? Didn't he tell you?" Natalie answered with silence and Nora caught the hint. "Well, I'm sure it's nothing. He'll call you later."

No, he won't, Natalie thought fighting tears, sensing whatever she'd hoped was blossoming between them was gone. She turned so Nora didn't see how devastated she felt. "I don't have much here. Most of it's upstairs."

"Okay," Nora said, moving toward the door, then stopping with a sudden thought. "Hey, am I supposed to get a wheelchair for you or something? Cuz I sure as hell can't carry you."

Natalie shot her sister a dark look. "Knock it off. As long as I don't try to lift anything heavier than a pencil, everything should be fine."

Nora arched an eyebrow. "And how do you know this?"

"I've been doing some reading on the Internet," she answered with a sigh. "Let's go," she urged, more interested in getting out of Evan's apartment than arguing with Nora about the virtues of the information superhighway.

As Natalie closed the door behind her, she couldn't help but feel that she'd just closed the door on what could've been a great future. Now all they had between them was the baby. Tears stung her eyes and she moved past Nora without looking back.

NORA CHEWED ON the inside of her cheek, trying not to worry. "He'll be back," she insisted, making a mental note to kill Evan if he made a liar out of her. "It's only been a few weeks."

"Yeah, and not one phone call in all that time," Natalie retorted, using anger to cover the hurt Nora knew was underneath. "He bailed. Plain and simple. He said he'd be back in a week. But it's been four weeks since then. How could I be so stupid?"

The last part ended with a wobble in her sister's voice and Nora amended her previous thought. She *was* going to kill Evan Murphy. "Well, he still has a lease on the apartment, he has to come back sometime," Nora offered, knowing even as she said it, it was weak. Natalie's shoulders sagged and she buried her face in her hands. Nora rushed to her side and tried wrapping her arms around her, which was difficult due to her enormous belly. "Please don't cry, Nat. You don't need this kind of stress. Besides, it's not like you had any serious feelings for the guy, right?" she asked, hoping her gut instinct was wrong. Natalie emitted a mournful wail that broke Nora's heart and all she could do was rock her. "I'm so sorry, Nat. I thought he might be *the one*. If I'd known he was going to cut out and run I would've never encouraged anything between you two."

"It's not your fault. I'm the one who fell in love with him," Natalie said, pulling away and wiping at her nose. "I didn't mean to. It just sort of happened when I wasn't paying attention."

The sneaky bastard. Nora made a mental note to be extra vigilant the next time she was attracted to someone. Attraction leads to heartache in this family, she thought darkly. The tears started again and Nora searched wildly for a change in subject. "Honey, don't waste another minute thinking about him. Think about the bookstore instead. It looks fabulous, by the way. I think your grand opening is going to be fantastic. People are already talking about it." She glanced out the window at the threatening sky with a mutinous frown and mumbled mostly to herself. "Now if only the weather will hold. If it rains…"

Natalie looked up, her face streaked with tears. "Really?" she asked with a loud sniff. "People are saying things? What exactly are they saying?"

Relieved to see her tactic worked, she eagerly relayed comments she'd picked up around town. "Oh, well, that's easy. I've heard people say that from the windows it looks pretty freaking amazing, the best children's bookstore around. In fact, I wouldn't doubt if you had standing room only next week."

Natalie swallowed and a tremulous smile followed. "That'd be nice. It was a lot of work," she admitted. "I don't think I could do it again. My lower back is killing me."

"Is everything ready? Do you need any more help?"

"No, everything's in place," Natalie answered, wiping the last of her tears away. "The books are inventoried and all I'm waiting for are the fake candle sconces that look like the ones you'd find in a castle. They were on backorder but they should arrive before next week."

"Excellent," Nora said, wishing she could clear away the dark circles under her sister's eyes and take away her heartache. She couldn't believe she'd been wrong about Evan. Usually she was a really good judge of character. How could she have been so far off base with him? A small voice wondered if they were jumping to the wrong conclusion but a louder voice reminded her that no matter where he'd gone, she was pretty sure they had telephone service. The fact that he hasn't called didn't weigh well in his favor. It was official: if she saw the miscreant again she'd land a left hook to his jaw for breaking her sister's soft heart. "Want to stay here tonight?" she asked. "We can rent some movies and pig out on Ding Dongs and Ho Hos."

Natalie offered a wan smile and shook her head. "As tempting as that sounds…I need to get home. Thanks, though. I should really get going before it gets too late. I'm pretty tired."

"Sure," Nora said, following Natalie to the door. "But if you need anything, don't hesitate to call, okay?"

Natalie nodded and climbed into her car.

As she watched her sister drive off, Nora worried about the effect stress was having on her pregnancy. Although she'd been removed from bed rest, Natalie was still in a precarious position. She wished to hell she knew where Evan was. One thing was for sure—if he showed up at the grand opening like nothing was wrong, she wouldn't have to deck him, Natalie would probably beat her to it.

CHAPTER TWENTY-THREE

THE DAY OF the grand opening broke with sunny skies despite the meteorologist's prediction that rain was certain to fall. Natalie sent a silent thank-you to the weather god and hurriedly grabbed her stuff to leave. With a mental list running in her head, she bent to grab her purse and groaned when the twinge in her back that had kept her awake all night blossomed into an even bigger spasm that took her breath away. Inhaling deeply, she rubbed at the painful spot and waited for it to pass. She made a mental note to talk to her doctor about it and locked up.

She had about an hour before the grand opening was scheduled to start and the wall sconces she'd been anxiously awaiting had only arrived yesterday toward the end of the workday. Moving as quickly as a woman carrying an extra forty pounds out in front could possibly manage, she ripped open the boxes and rushed to find her electric screwdriver. She could do this. Nothing was going to stand in her way of making this bookstore a complete success. After locating the screwdriver she pulled the small step stool from the supply closet and set about placing the sconces. With screws clamped firmly between her lips, she focused on getting the job done. The bell above the door tinkled and she turned in surprise, wondering if her clock was off.

The screws dropped from her mouth and rolled to the floor as she stared. Her heart thundered to a near stop and her whole body went on heightened alert.

Evan.

"Are you supposed to be on that?" he asked with a concerned frown.

For a second she ignored his question and just drank in his appearance. He certainly didn't look as if he'd been in mortal danger, which was the only scenario she could think of that would've possibly prevented him from making a simple phone call. Although, she noted with reluctance, he did look a little ragged around the edges, as if he hadn't slept well. Just as her mouth opened to ask if he was all right, her brain registered the censure in Evan's voice and she snapped back to reality. *As if he had the right to even care!* Anger burst in hot lavalike splashes all over her insides, ready to boil over and incinerate him, but luck was on his side. A glance at the clock revealed she didn't have time to eviscerate him, as she would've liked to. She straightened and stepped down, bending to retrieve the lost screws. "What are you doing here? I don't remember inviting you," she said coolly. "You still have time to leave before my family arrives and beats you into the ground."

He reached for her as she walked by and she sidestepped, avoiding his touch as if it were the plague. "Don't."

The one word, coupled with the glare, stopped him, but she could tell it wasn't going to be enough to make him leave. When it suited him, he was the definition of tenacity.

"Natalie, let me explain."

Laughter bubbled up inside her but she didn't much feel like laughing. In fact, a scream echoing all the pain she'd been going through since he left would've been her choice if given one. Fortunately, she recognized shrieking at the top of her lungs would only scare away future customers and swallowed the impulse. Instead, she spared Evan a frosty glower and continued with her tasks as if her heart wasn't alternately breaking and rejoicing at his presence. "Explaining would've been effective three weeks ago. Today, it's just pointless."

"I know you're mad," he conceded gently, daring to take a step forward, his eyes warm and beautiful and the last thing Natalie wanted to see. "Natalie, please listen and I'll explain everything."

"No." She turned away and drew a deep breath. "Get out."

"Not until you hear me out."

"Why? Why should I do that when you left me like a coward?"

He had the grace to look guilty and she started to soften toward him, wanting to hear his explanation, hoping it would dispel the awful knot building under her breastbone and making her nauseous.

"I know that's how it probably looks but I didn't think I'd be gone so long."

She stared. That was his explanation? He lost track of time? *Jackass*. She turned, renewed anger burning away any burgeoning shreds of understanding that may have begun when he started. His voice at her back made her pause. "I got a job."

"Bully for you," Natalie retorted, whirling around. Why did he have to wear such a hopeful expression? Didn't he see she had nothing but spite left for him? Her mouth tightened against the urge to ask for details. She wouldn't care. He left her. How much more simple did it need to be?

"Bully for me?" he repeated in openmouthed shock. "Wasn't that your big concern? That I didn't have a 'real' job?"

"Not the only concern," she answered starchily, lifting her chin. "There were many. But I can see how that would be the one point you'd center on. You taking off like you did just proved to me that you're not ready to be a father." His brown eyes darkened and Natalie almost wished she could take it back, but all she'd done was state the facts. Surely, he recognized that. Still, her voice lost some of its rancor as she continued, "How can I trust that you won't pull another disappearing act when I need you the most? When our son needs you?"

"I didn't want to come back until I had something to offer you!" he nearly shouted, startling her into open-mouthed shock. He tugged on a wayward curl at the back of his neck and looked away, angry. When he swiveled back to her, his expression morphed into one bordering on humiliation. "Like I said…it took longer than I anticipated. Seems there aren't all that many jobs for those with my bohemian background. My degree got me in the door but when they learned I had zero practical application, the opportunities dried up quickly."

"But why couldn't you just call me and tell me that?" she asked, her tone almost a frustrated wail at his decision to stay away for such a dumb reason. "You could've given me the chance to be there for you. Instead, you locked me out. I'm afraid it'll always be like that and I need more."

"I know that. And I want to give you more!" he insisted, moving toward her until she took a step away, sending the clear message she couldn't let her yearning for his touch cloud her judgment. He frowned but he didn't press it. "Why is it so hard for you to believe what I'm saying to you?"

Because if I believe you, I'll have to compromise myself. Unwelcome tears filled her eyes. "What was her name?" she asked, somehow knowing a woman was behind his reluctance to make a commitment.

"What?" he said, confused. "Who?"

"The woman who broke your heart," she answered, attempting to cross her arms across her chest. "Obviously, someone did a number on you to make you act the way you do. Afraid of commitment and all that."

Evan hesitated. "That's old news. I'm over it."

"Sure you are."

She turned away, but he caught her arm gently. Evan's beseeching gaze infuriated her further and she jerked herself free. When he realized she wasn't going to give in without the information she demanded, he swore.

"Hailey. Her name was Hailey. She was my fiancée."

"What happened between you two?"

"Oh, c'mon! What difference does that make?" His pained expression might've softened her before his disappearing act but at the moment she felt like stone. Blowing a hard breath, he looked away as if he couldn't bear to look her in the eye as he explained. "She left me for my best friend right after college. She was pregnant but didn't know whose kid it was and aborted," he said, his voice filled with bitterness.

"That's why you couldn't walk away," she whispered, his shoulders stiffened as understanding dawned and Natalie breathed against the sharp pain in her chest. "From our baby. From me."

"At first…yes," he admitted. "But it's different now. I realize what I had with Hailey was an illusion." He thumped on his chest. "What I feel here is real."

She desperately wanted to believe him. If only he hadn't left her dangling in the wind, wondering where he'd gone. One simple phone call could've circumvented all of this heartache but he hadn't believed in her enough to take that chance. If he had…they might've had a chance. God knows, she loved him. That wasn't the problem.

Deliberately hardening her voice, she said, "I'm sorry you were hurt but if this is some last-ditch effort to ensure that you're not excluded from your child, save it. Your paternity is not at stake. I won't keep your son from you." She drew a deep, shuddering breath but didn't meet his incredulous stare. *You can do this.* One word after another makes a sentence and it'll soon be over. Better now than later when you've come to depend on him. Damn him for letting her fall in love with him. He should've tried harder to keep the lines drawn so neither one ended up brokenhearted. Scratch that. It seems she was the only one fighting tears at the moment. She straightened. "Leave me a number and I'll make sure someone calls you when the baby is born. We'll work out the custody exchanges later. Right now I have to focus on the bookstore."

"Natalie—"

She turned, exasperation coloring her voice. "Are you deaf? I said I don't want to hear it!" she nearly shouted, her chest heaving. "I have an opening in less than fifteen minutes and I don't have time to listen to your juvenile excuses about why you left without saying goodbye and why you couldn't even pick up a *damn* phone to tell me what was going on! Now, get out!" She pointed to the door with an emphatic motion until another pain zeroed in on her lower back, causing her to double over. This time the pain radiated from her back to form a band around her belly and she gasped against the searing hot agony.

"Natalie?" Evan was instantly by her side but she batted him away. Fear made his voice urgent. "Natalie, stop it. What's wrong? Where does it hurt?"

"None…of…your…business!" She managed to say between gritted teeth. Nora was supposed to be there any minute. She just had to hold out until then. Evan slipped his arms around her for support, and as much as she wanted to shrug off his touch, another wave hit her and she leaned into him with a fearful groan. Not now! "Evan? Something's wrong…"

By the look on his face, he didn't disagree and quickly scooped her in his arms as if she didn't weigh a ton. Carefully placing her in the truck, he slammed the door and rounded the other side just as Nora pulled up and jumped out.

"What's going on?" she asked, moving so quickly she almost stumbled when she reached Evan's truck. Natalie groaned as she clutched her stomach and Nora paled several shades. "Oh, no," she breathed, the panic in her voice mirroring what Natalie was feeling inside. "I'll be right behind you!"

"No…stay," Natalie gasped, gesturing to the store. "I need…someone here. Please!"

Nora gave a reluctant nod though it was clear she wanted to follow them to the hospital. Natalie tried reassuring her with a tight smile as she gritted her teeth against the pain. "I'll be fine. It's probably…nothing," The last part came out in a guttural moan and Evan gunned the engine. Natalie cast a mournful look at her bookstore, noting that people were starting to arrive, just as she was leaving.

NORA PACED. Evan was back in town. But Natalie was in labor. Preterm labor, at that. What was he thinking? Was he crazy to show his face after what he pulled? But what if there was more to the story than met the eye? She slapped a hand to her head, groaning at the incessant chatter of questions running through her head. The bell above the door sounded and she glanced at the clock with dawning terror.

She was going to have to play hostess while her sister was giving birth. Oh, crap.

"Welcome to the Dragon's Lair," she said, forcing a smile even though it probably looked as fake as the medieval wall sconces. "I'm Nora, my sister Natalie is actually in labor right now so she couldn't be here but she'd like you to enjoy the grand opening in her absence!" Murmurs of surprise and concern rumbled through the crowd as more and more people, most toting children, filed into the charming bookstore. As a last effort to play hostess, she gestured toward the table laden with cookies, cakes and all sorts of gooey goodies that Nora would've never encouraged in a bookstore. As she lifted the cell phone to her ear, she said, "Help yourself to the stuff over there. I don't know what it is but I'm sure it's good. Natalie's scoped out every bakery from here to Coldwater to satisfy her weird cravings. So…enjoy!"

Now, she had the unenviable job of calling their parents. As she dialed, she muttered, "Some days it just doesn't pay to get out of bed!"

EVAN PULLED INTO the hospital emergency parking and made quick work of getting

Natalie from the car into the hospital. He shouted for help and nurses came running.

Natalie whimpered, the sound tearing into his heart, as she clutched at her stomach. She looked up at him, tears sparkling in her eyes, her arm tightening around his neck. "Don't leave," she begged and he shook his head.

"I'm not going anywhere," he promised, giving the charge nurse a steely look when she appeared about ready to take Natalie and send him to the waiting room.

"Put her in exam room two," the nurse ordered and pointed. "We'll send someone in right away."

Evan helped her to the bed and a doctor appeared shortly after.

"Where does it hurt?" he asked, getting straight to the point.

"My lower back," she answered, gritting her teeth and trying to breathe against the pain.

"When did it start?"

"Last night, maybe? I'm not sure. It just got really bad about fifteen minutes ago."

A nurse appeared with an odd cart filled with things Evan couldn't readily identify, but he figured it was something for the baby.

When the nurse exposed Natalie's belly and wrapped a soft belt with a monitor around her stomach, he realized his guess was correct. Within minutes, a graph started charting little mountains across the page. The doctor paused long enough to study the paper, then nodded.

"You're in preterm labor, Ms. Simmons," he announced. "How far along are you?"

"Just about nine months, but it's too early, isn't it?" she protested, sending Evan a panicked look. "I'm not due until March eighth."

"We will try to stop your labor but judging by these contractions, I don't think we'll be successful."

"Is the baby going to be all right…if he's born early?" Evan swallowed the lump in his throat, knowing Natalie needed him to be strong. "He's going to be okay, right?"

"Typically, a baby's lungs at this stage of the gestation are fine but we won't know for sure until he gets here. Try to rest. Use your breathing techniques and we will bring you something for the pain while your room is prepared."

The doctor left and the nurse turned to them with a kindly face. "I'm sure it'll be fine. This is a fetal monitor. It will tell us how many contractions you're having and the intensity, but it will also tell us if the baby is in distress. Right now, your baby looks fine but I agree with the doctor—I think you're going to be parents sooner rather than later."

She smiled warmly and Evan took hope in that. Natalie inhaled sharply and his attention was drawn to the monitor. Sure enough, as Natalie's hand tightened on his own—almost to the point he was sure his knuckles were going to splinter—the little needle rose steeply, drawing a jagged mountain across the paper. "Guess it's too late to take Lamaze classes now, huh?" he asked, half-seriously. She surprised him with a short smile, but it faded quickly as another wave hit her. She groaned and her hold tightened. Holy crap, she could crack walnuts with that grip!

A different nurse returned and set about putting an IV together.

"This should help with the pain, hun," the nurse explained as she tapped a vein and expertly inserted the needle, taping it to Natalie's arm carefully so it didn't get dislodged. "Just give it a minute and it'll take the edge off."

"Thank you," she said in a low, tortured voice.

"Yes, thank you," Evan echoed gratefully, not quite sure he'd ever have full use of his hand again after this experience.

Moments later, Natalie exhaled slowly and her whole body relaxed. "Meds kick in?" he asked gently and she nodded.

"Better. Much better." She gestured weakly. "Make sure that very sweet nurse has a bunch of whatever she just put in my IV. I don't think I can handle labor without it."

"I pegged you as the type who'd want nothing but natural labor, as in no drugs," he teased, coaxing a brief but guarded smile from her. The small gesture filled him with optimism and he dragged a chair to sit beside her. "How are you feeling?" he asked when she twisted and a low groan followed.

"Hurts still," she mumbled, her eyelids drooping. To his surprise, within moments she was out. He reached over and gently pushed her golden hair away from her eyes, the texture like silk as it slid through his fingers. Somehow he had to convince her that his absence had been for a good cause, even if he didn't call. After the first week, coming up with nothing, embarrassment had kept him from picking up the phone. He couldn't return without success.

An hour later she stirred, eyes fluttering open, wracked with pain and he knew whatever reprieve had been afforded by the medication was coming to an end.

"Ev-an," she groaned, her face scrunching in a mask of pain. "I can't take it."

He crowded closer. "Yes, you can. I know you can."

Tears shimmered in her eyes as she shook her head. Locking onto her fearful stare, he coaxed her with a gentle but firm voice to breathe through the pain. "*You* breathe through the pain," she snapped bitterly but made an effort to take slower, more even breaths. "This isn't fair," she gasped, clenching his hand with her own. "I was supposed to have another month!"

Don't I know it, he agreed wryly. He'd hoped to have everything squared away and in place by the time their son arrived. Now, it seems his birth was going to follow the pattern of his creation: unexpected and wild. In spite of the circumstances, a grin tugged at his mouth, earning a frown from Natalie even as she panted and blew in an attempt to deal with the pain. "What's so funny?" she practically growled.

"I'll tell you later," he promised, knowing right now her sense of humor was on hiatus. Before she could retort, another sharp pain hit her and the groan she'd started with erupted into a screech.

"Get the doctor, *now!*"

Evan scrambled from her side, shouting as he went. "I need help in here!" He turned a corner and nearly ran over Natalie's parents.

"What are you doing here?" Gerald growled in time for Nora to skid around the corner, breathing heavily.

"Damn, I was trying to beat them," she said between gasps. "Boy, I'm out of shape." She straightened and poked her father in the shoulder. "And you drive way too fast for a man your age. You could've taken out a squadron of kids in a crosswalk or something."

Missy interjected in annoyance, "Nora, please! You're not helping."

"I said you weren't welcome in this family," Gerald barked, stabbing a finger at Evan as he aimed to push him back. But Evan held his ground, too charged with adrenaline to bother with trying to be polite. Besides, it wasn't like the old man was trying all that hard to censor his words. "Where's my daughter?" he nearly shouted until Missy put a hand on his arm with a warning look.

"Yeah, Dad, we are in a hospital. You know that place where sick people go for a little rest!" Nora quipped.

"Nora, shut up for once!" Missy exclaimed, shocking Nora into guilty silence though she did send Evan a look that said "good luck" before stalking past them to the nurse's desk.

"Listen," he said curtly when Gerald opened his mouth to bluster some more, "I love your daughter and right now she's down the hall having my baby. Do you hear me? *My baby*. And that ain't going to change. Nor does the fact that I plan to stick around for the next fifty or so years. So unless you want to spend those years glaring at each other from across the Thanksgiving dinner table, get used to it."

"Gerald?" Missy tugged at his sleeve and he spared her a grudging glance. "It's Natalie's choice," she reminded him, her gentle voice surprisingly firm. Gerald held his wife's stare for a long moment, no doubt weighing her words, then turned back to Evan.

"You love her?"

"I do," he answered solemnly.

Gerald's mouth tightened as he came to an inevitable conclusion. For a wild second Evan was afraid the gauntlet he'd thrown was going to backfire, but finally, Gerald conceded, although not before adding, "You break her heart and you'll answer to me."

"Fair enough," he said, moving away, anxious to get back to looking for a doctor, but Missy stepped forward with worry etched on her face.

"Can we see her?"

"I think she'd like that." He offered a silent thank-you for her gentle persuasion and told them where to find Natalie's room. Seconds later he was running back down the hall, searching for someone who resembled a doctor.

Careening into the first white coat he saw, he grabbed at the poor man and practically dragged him back to Natalie's room. Nora, Gerald and Missy were crowded into the small room, each wearing a fretful expression, until a nurse pushed past them to check Natalie's vitals. A suggestion was made to clear the room and everyone filed out with a promise to wait in the waiting room.

The young man, irritated by Evan's behavior, shrugged out of Evan's tight grip, his pimpled face wrinkled in displeasure until Natalie's shriek turned into an unearthly grunt as she strained so hard her face started to purple. They both turned and stared. The woman Evan wanted to spend the rest of his life with was turning into a she-beast right before his very eyes. Was this normal? Gesturing wildly, he shouted, "Help her, man!"

Recovering quickly, the young man stammered, "I'm not a doctor! I work in the lab! But I think that chick's about to have a baby!" *Way to grab the brainiac!* Evan ignored the man as he fled the room, and returned to Natalie's side, feeling more helpless than he'd ever been in his life. He smoothed her hair from her face until she jerked away, annoyed with the contact. "What do you want me to do?" he asked, looking for direction. *Tell me something so I don't feel as useless as tits on a boar!*

"Make the pain stop!" she demanded, right before she bore down again.

"Are you...pushing?" he asked, incredulous. He looked around nervously. Where the hell was the doctor? "I'm not sure if you're supposed—"

"Shut up, Evan!" Her voice deepened with the strain. "When you have a bowling ball trying to come out your private parts you can tell me what I'm supposed to do...until then—*shut the hell up!*"

Where was that lovely nurse with all the drugs? he wondered in a haze, wiping the sweat beading on his forehead. Just then the doctor entered with a grin that if he'd worn it Natalie would've snarled at his nerve. But at the sight of the doctor, she offered a brief, pained smile as she realized relief would come soon.

After a quick check, the doctor smiled from over the top of Natalie's knees and started slipping on latex gloves. "You are a champion birther," he noted enthusiastically and Natalie thanked him for the dubious compliment with a loud grunt. "A few more good pushes, and you'll have your baby."

The nursing staff buzzed around Evan as they readied the room for the imminent birth of his son, and he didn't know whether to be scared, excited or plain freaked out at the fact that within moments, he was going to become a father.

"I want drugs," she managed to gasp and the doctor had the gall to chuckle.

"Too late for that." He peered down at her nether region and a satisfied smile broke. "Now really get serious and *push!*"

Get serious? Evan wanted to shout for Natalie's sake. What the heck did the guy think the poor woman had been doing for the past hour? Playing around? He didn't have long to berate him for his choice of words, because Natalie did exactly that and the doctor exclaimed, "Good job! We have a head! A full head of dark hair by the looks of it!"

Dark hair? He peered around Natalie's knee and caught the first look of his son, just as the next push sent him sliding free with a gush of fluid and a relieved sigh rattled out of Natalie. The doctor quickly handed the small, wrinkled bundle to the nurses standing by. "It's a boy," the doctor announced unnecessarily, returning his attention to Natalie who, just like Evan, was trying hard to catch a glimpse of the small boy who was swamped by a team of pediatric nurses.

"Is he all right?" he heard Natalie ask in a hoarse whisper. She turned to Evan, fear and uncertainty in her bloodshot eyes. "Why isn't he crying?"

"I don't know," he answered, pressing a quick kiss to her crown. *Please be okay.* "I'm sure he's fine."

As if God heard his silent plea, his son finally let out a lusty squall that was music to his ears. The baby continued to voice his displeasure and the doctor chuckled. "He may be early but if he can yowl like that I think his lungs are probably A-OK. But, just to be on the safe side, they're going to have to take him down to the NICU. You can see him after they make sure he's going to be able to breathe on his own."

His son. That was his son they were working on. Tears overflowed his eyes and sentiment choked the air out of his lungs. In all his life he'd never forget this moment. He stared down at Natalie, limp and ragged, and wondered if he'd ever seen anyone look so beautiful.

Natalie closed her eyes while the doctor finished. Evan moistened a washcloth and pressed it against her damp crown, garnering her gratitude. She opened her eyes. "You can go with him," she offered, but he shook his head emphatically. "Why not?" she asked, confused.

He smiled, knowing he was right where he belonged and the only place he'd ever want to be. "Because I know he's in good hands and when we go to see our son...we'll do it together." Tears welled in her eyes and he was hard-pressed to hold back his own, but he grasped her hand and held it to his chest as he struggled to voice what he was feeling inside. "I love you, Natalie. That's what I was trying to tell you." Tears flowed openly down her cheeks and she accepted his tender kiss. "Without you I'm half a man and, contrary to what you may have thought, I'll gladly spend the rest of our lives proving to you that I am father material because—" he leaned forward and whispered so only she could hear "—I plan to be the father of *all* your children. Now and forever. I promise."

She stared hard, mindless of the tears streaming down her face and he held her gaze. Finally, a slow fatigued smile spread across her face and she nodded in relief as she wrapped her arms around his neck and pulled him the final distance to her lips. "That's a promise I'm going to hold you to," she murmured, her voice a husky whisper against his flesh as her mouth curved around the sweetest word in the English language. "Daddy."

EPILOGUE

COLTON JEREMIAH MURPHY was a beautiful child, everyone agreed. Golden curls replaced the dark, newborn hair of his birth and dark brown eyes stared with curious intelligence that surely bespoke a future genius to hear Evan tell it.

"Evan," Nora groaned as she rocked her nephew to sleep so Natalie could grab a bite to eat. "Every parent thinks their kid is the best. You're no different." But she belied her words by pressing a kiss on the top of Colton's head, making Natalie smile around the big bite of potato salad in her mouth. Nora shrugged as if she'd been caught. "Well, he does seem pretty smart for his age."

"Of course he's smart. He's a Simmons!"

Gerald interjected. "And if he's anything like his grandpop he'll be a stellar athlete."

Nora smothered her groan but couldn't contain the impulse to roll her eyes. "Dad, golf isn't what I'd consider a true sport."

"Why not? It takes endurance, accuracy… Have you ever tried your hand at it?"

Natalie sighed, listening to the bickering between Nora and their father, and enjoyed the fact that she no longer felt the need to referee their conversations. She glanced at her mother, who was watching Nora with Colton, her eyes shining with love…and tears.

"Mom? You all right?"

Missy swiveled her gaze over to Natalie and a smile broke out. "We have a lot to be thankful for and no matter what the future holds…I want to remember this moment forever."

Natalie understood exactly how she felt. She and Evan were getting ready to buy their first house. Colton brought unparalleled joy to their life and The Dragon's Lair was so successful she'd already hired someone to help part-time. A swell of contentment filled her emotional cup to overflowing and she was glad to share. Turning to her mother, she placed her hand atop hers and sent her a smile, full with happiness, and said, "Me, too, Mom. Me, too."

* * * * *

*Natalie and Nora's sister, Tasha,
is coming home to Emmett's Mill.
Be sure to look for Tasha's story
in February 2008, wherever
Harlequin books are sold!*

**Every Life Has More
Than One Chapter™**

Award-winning author Stevi Mittman
delivers another hysterical mystery, featuring
Teddi Bayer, an irrepressible heroine, and
her to-die-for hero, Detective Drew Scoones.
After all, life on Long Island can be murder!

*Turn the page for a sneak peek
at the warm and funny fourth book,
WHOSE NUMBER IS UP, ANYWAY?,
in the Teddi Bayer series,
by STEVI MITTMAN.
On sale August 7*

"Before redecorating a room, I always advise my clients to empty it of everything but one chair. Then I suggest they move that chair from place to place, sitting in it, until the placement feels right. Trust your instincts when deciding on furniture placement. Your room should 'feel right.'"

—TipsFromTeddi.com

Gut feelings. You know, that gnawing in the pit of your stomach that warns you that you are about to do the absolute stupidest thing you could do? Something that will ruin life as you know it?

I've got one now, standing at the butcher counter in King Kullen, the grocery store in the same strip mall as L.I. Lanes, the bowling alley cum billiard parlor I'm in the process of redecorating for its "Grand Opening."

I realize being in the wrong supermarket probably doesn't sound exactly dire to you, but you aren't the one buying your father a brisket at a store your mother will somehow know isn't Waldbaum's.

And then, June Bayer isn't your mother.

The woman behind the counter has agreed to go into the freezer to find a brisket for me, since there aren't any in the case. There are packages of pork tenderloin, piles of spare ribs and rolls of sausage, but no briskets.

Warning Number Two, right? I should be so out of here.

But no, I'm still in the same spot when she comes back out, brisketless, her face ashen. She opens her mouth as if she is going to scream, but only a gurgle comes out.

And then she pinballs out from behind the counter, knocking bottles of Peter Luger Steak Sauce to the floor on her way, now hitting the tower of cans at the end of the prepared foods aisle and sending them sprawling, now making her way down the aisle, careening from side to side as she goes.

Finally, from a distance, I hear her shout, "He's deeeeeeaaaad! Joey's deeeeeaaaad."

My first thought is *You should always trust your gut*.

My second thought is that now, somehow, my mother will know I was in King Kullen. For weeks I will have to hear "What did you expect?" as though whenever you go to King Kullen someone turns up dead. And if the detective investigating the case turns out to be Detective Drew Scoones…well, I'll never hear the end of that from her, either.

She still suspects I murdered the guy who was found dead on my doorstep last Halloween just to get Drew back into my life.

Several people head for the butcher's freezer and I position myself to block them. If there's one thing I've learned from finding people dead—and the guy on my doorstep wasn't the first one—it's that the police get very testy when you mess with their murder scenes.

"You can't go in there until the police get here," I say, stationing myself at the end of the butcher's counter and in front of the Employees Only door, acting as if I'm some sort of authority. "You'll contaminate the evidence if it turns out to be murder."

Shouts and chaos. You'd think I'd know better than to throw the word *murder* around. Cell phones are flipping open and tongues are wagging.

I amend my statement quickly. "Which, of course, it probably isn't. Murder, I mean. People die all the time, and it's not always in hospitals or their own beds, or…" I babble when I'm nervous, and the idea of someone dead on the other side of the freezer door makes me very nervous.

So does the idea of seeing Drew Scoones again. Drew and I have this on-again, off-again sort of thing…that I kind of turned off.

Who knew he'd take it so personally when he tried to get serious and I responded by saying we could talk about *us* tomorrow—and then caught a plane to my parents' condo in Boca the next day? In July. In the middle of a job.

For some crazy reason, he took that to mean that I was avoiding him and the subject of *us*.

That was three months ago. I haven't seen him since.

The manager, who identifies himself and points to his nameplate in case I don't believe him, says he has to go into *his cooler*.

"Maybe Joey's not dead," he says. "Maybe he can be saved, and you're letting him die in there. Did you ever think of that?"

In fact, I hadn't. But I had thought that the murderer might try to go back in to make sure his tracks were covered, so I say that I will go in and check.

Which means that the manager and I couple up and go in together while everyone pushes against the doorway to peer in, erasing any chance of finding clean prints on that Employee Only door.

I expect to find carcasses of dead animals hanging from hooks, and maybe Joey hanging from one, too. I think it's going to be very creepy and I steel myself, only to find a rather benign series of shelves with large slabs of meat laid out carefully on them, along with boxes and boxes marked simply Chicken.

Nothing scary here, unless you count the body of a middle-aged man with graying hair sprawled faceup on the floor. His eyes are wide open and unblinking. His shirt is stiff. His pants are stiff. His body is stiff. And his expression, you should forgive the pun—is frozen. Bill-the-manager crosses himself and stands mute while I pronounce the guy dead in a sort of *happy now?* tone.

"We should not be in here," I say, and he nods his head emphatically and helps me push people out of the doorway just in time to hear the police sirens and see the cop cars pull up outside the big store windows.

Bobbie Lyons, my partner in Teddi Bayer Interior Designs (and also my neighbor, my best friend and my private fashion police), and Mark, our carpenter (and my dogsitter, confidant and ego booster), rush in from next door. They beat the cops by a half step and shout out my name. People point in my direction.

After all the publicity that followed the unfortunate incident during which I shot my ex-husband, Rio Gallo, and then the subsequent murder of my first client—which I solved, I might add—it seems like the whole world, or at least all of Long Island, knows who I am.

Mark asks if I'm all right. (Did I remember to mention that the man is drop-dead-gorgeous-but-a-decade-too-young-for-me-yet-too-old-for-my-daughter-thank-god?) I don't get a chance to answer him because the police are quickly closing in on the store manager and me.

"The woman—" I begin telling the police. Then I have to pause for the manager to fill in her name, which he does: *Fran*.

I continue. "Right. Fran. Fran went into the freezer to get a brisket. A moment later she came out and screamed that Joey was dead. So I'd say she was the one who discovered the body."

"And you are…?" the cop asks me. It comes out a bit like who do I *think* I am, rather than who am I really?

"An innocent bystander," Bobbie, hair perfect, makeup just right, says, carefully placing her body between the cop and me.

"And she was just leaving," Mark adds. They each take one of my arms.

Fran comes into the inner circle surrounding the cops. In case it isn't obvious from the hairnet and bloodstained white apron with Fran embroidered on it, I explain that she was the butcher who was going for the brisket. Mark and Bobbie take that as a signal that I've done my job and they can now get me out of there. They twist around, with me in the middle, as if we're a Rockettes line, until we are facing away from the butcher counter. They've managed to propel me a few steps toward the exit when disaster—in the form of a Mazda RX7 pulling up at the loading curb—strikes.

Mark's grip on my arm tightens like a vise. "Too late," he says.

Bobbie's expletive is unprintable. "Maybe there's a back door," she suggests, but Mark is right. It's too late.

I've laid my eyes on Detective Scoones. And while my gut is trying to warn me that my heart shouldn't go there, regions farther south are melting at just the sight of him.

"Walk," Bobbie orders me.

And I try to. Really.

Walk, I tell my feet. *Just put one foot in front of the other.*

I can do this because I know, in my heart of hearts, that if Drew Scoones was still interested in me, he'd have gotten in touch with me after I returned from Boca. And he didn't.

Since he's a detective, Drew doesn't have to wear one of those dark blue Nassau County Police uniforms. Instead, he's got on jeans, a tight-fitting T-shirt and a tweedy sports jacket. If you think that sounds good, you should see him. Chiseled features, cleft chin, brown hair that's naturally a little sandy in the front, a smile that…well, that doesn't matter. He isn't smiling now.

He walks up to me, tucks his sunglasses into his breast pocket and looks me over from head to toe.

"Well, if it isn't Miss Cut and Run," he says. "Aren't you supposed to be somewhere in Florida or something?" He looks at Mark accusingly, as if he was covering for me when he told Drew I was gone.

"Detective Scoones?" one of the uniforms says. "The stiff's in the cooler and the woman who found him is over there." He jerks his head in Fran's direction.

Drew continues to stare at me.

You know how when you were young, your mother always told you to wear clean underwear in case you were in an accident? And how, a little farther on, she told you not to go out in hair rollers because you never knew who you might see—or who might see you? And how now your best friend says she wouldn't be caught dead without makeup and suggests you shouldn't either?

Okay, today, *finally,* in my overalls and Converse sneakers, I get it.

I brush my hair out of my eyes. "Well, I'm

back," I say. As if he hasn't known my exact whereabouts. The man is a detective, for heaven's sake. "Been back awhile."

Bobbie has watched the exchange and apparently decided she's given Drew all the time he deserves. "And we've got work to do, so…" she says, grabbing my arm and giving Drew a little two-fingered wave goodbye.

As I back up a foot or two, the store manager sees his chance and places himself in front of Drew, trying to get his attention. Maybe what makes Drew such a good detective is his ability to focus.

Only what he's focusing on is me.

"Phone broken? Carrier pigeon died?" he asks me, taking in Fran, the manager, the meat counter and that Employees Only door, all without taking his eyes off me.

Mark tries to break the spell. "We've got work to do there, you've got work to do here, Scoones," Mark says to him, gesturing toward next door. "So it's back to the alley for us."

Drew's lip twitches. "You working the alley now?" he says.

"If you'd like to follow me," Bill-the-manager, clearly exasperated, says to

Drew—who doesn't respond. It's as if waiting for my answer is all he has to do.

So, fine. "You knew I was back," I say.

The man has known my whereabouts every hour of the day for as long as I've known him. And my mother's not the only one who won't buy that he "just happened" to answer this particular call. In fact, I'm willing to bet my children's lunch money that he's taken every call within ten miles of my home since the day I got back.

And now he's gotten lucky.

"*You* could have called *me*," I say.

"You're the one who said *tomorrow* for our talk and then flew the coop, chickie," he says. "I figured the ball was in your court."

"Detective?" the uniform says. "There's something you ought to see in here."

Drew gives me a look that amounts to *in or out?*

He could be talking about the investigation, or about our relationship.

Bobbie tries to steer me away. Mark's fists are balled. Drew waits me out, knowing I won't be able to resist what might be a murder investigation.

Finally he turns and heads for the cooler.

And, like a puppy dog, I follow.

Bobbie grabs the back of my shirt and pulls me to a halt.

"I'm just going to show him something," I say, yanking away.

"Yeah," Bobbie says, pointedly looking at the buttons on my blouse. The two at breast level have popped. "That's what I'm afraid of."

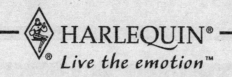

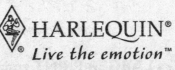

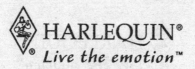

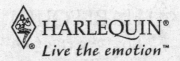

Harlequin® Historical
Historical Romantic Adventure!

*Imagine a time of chivalrous
knights and unconventional ladies,
roguish rakes and impetuous
heiresses, rugged cowboys
and spirited frontierswomen—
these rich and vivid tales will
capture your imagination!*

*Harlequin Historical...
they're too good to miss!*

HHDIR06

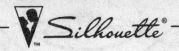

Silhouette ®

SPECIAL EDITION™

Emotional, compelling stories that capture the intensity of living, loving and creating a family in today's world.

Silhouette ®

Desire

Modern, passionate reads that are powerful and provocative.

Silhouette

nocturne

Dramatic and sensual tales of paranormal romance.

Silhouette Romantic

SUSPENSE

Romances that are sparked by danger and fueled by passion.

SDIR07